Rock 'n' Roll Nights

Rock 'n' Roll Nights

A Novel by
Todd Strasser

DELACORTE PRESS/NEW YORK

Published by
Delacorte Press
1 Dag Hammarskjold Plaza
New York, N.Y. 10017

Manufactured in the United States of America

First printing

Designed by Richard Oriolo

Library of Congress Cataloging in Publication Data

Strasser, Todd.
Rock 'n' roll nights.
Summary: High school rock musicians Gary, Susan, Oscar, and Karl, in a band known as the Electric Outlet, pursue their dream of stardom by trying to get their pictures in the paper and their records on the radio.
[1. Rock music—Fiction.   2. Musicians—Fiction]
I. Title.
PZ7.S889Ro   [Fic]   81-12618
ISBN 0-440-07407-X   AACR2

• For Pamela •

One

New York City, 6:00 A.M. Saturday morning. The sun was still below the horizon of buildings. The streets were empty and gray. In a dark apartment near Riverside Park, Gary Specter lay on a stranger's bed wondering how he had gotten there and how he could escape. The wooden blinds were drawn across the windows, and somewhere in that dark apartment was a woman named Kathy, whom he'd met a few hours ago in the smoky rock club where he and his band, the Electric Outlet, had performed. After the show, for some crazy reason, Gary had let her take him back to her apartment. He couldn't remember the reason now. All he knew was that he must have been out of his mind.

In the darkness Gary sensed someone moving toward him. The bed tipped and creaked. A hand reached in his direction. Gary backed away.

Truly, he'd gotten himself into some ludicrous situations in his life, but nothing in recent memory could match this. Not that Kathy didn't seem nice and everything, but she had to be a lot older than he to live alone in an apartment. College-aged at least. Couldn't she see that he was only a high school senior?

Apparently she couldn't, because the next thing Gary knew Kathy was crawling on top of him. As she pinned him beneath her, Gary realized he could no longer postpone what he had to say.

"Uh, we better not."

"What?" She sounded startled.

"I said, we better not," Gary repeated, bracing himself for who knew what kind of drunken, angry response.

But the body above him lay motionless on his chest, making it hard to breathe. Her lips were only a few inches from his face and the hot stench of cigarettes, booze, and unbrushed teeth rushed up his nose with every struggling breath. It was almost worth it not to breathe.

"Why not?" she asked.

"Because I don't love you," Gary said.

"But I don't love you either," she said.

"So we agree."

"You're not serious." She chuckled.

"I am," Gary whispered, wishing that she'd get off him.

"But, it doesn't make sense," she said, no longer chuckling.

"I know."

Above him, she pondered this. The steady supply of fermented, nicotine-flavored breath plus the pressure on his chest was making Gary dizzy, but he was afraid to ask her to move. More rejection would only lead to hostility. *Gary Specter and the Sensitive Heartbreakers.* Suddenly she slid off him and Gary took a deep, thankful breath.

"The first time in my life I pick up a rock musician," she sighed, "and he turns out to be a sickie."

"No, not a sickie," Gary said, "just . . ."

"Just what?"

Gary shrugged. How could he explain? An hour ago he *had* been a rock musician. He'd looked the part with his tall, slender build and his dark hair falling into his eyes. And he'd acted the part too, returning the gazes of the women in the audience with his own dark eyes, prancing across the stage, gyrating his hips, and caressing his guitar. But it was just an act. In the hour since they'd left the club together he'd been transformed. Like Cinderella's carriage turning back into a pumpkin, the stud rock star had turned back into a seventeen-year-old high school virgin.

Kathy reached across him in the dark and Gary heard the crinkle of cellophane. A small flame burst out of her hand and she touched it to a cigarette. In the flickering glow of the lighter she glanced at him for a moment and then let the flame die.

"Don't be mad," he said softly, pushing a few thick strands of hair out of his eyes.

"I just can't believe it," she replied. "You looked so sexy on the stage."

"I know." Gary sighed. He often practiced in front of a mirror.

The red embers of the cigarette glowed in the dark and Gary tried to imagine what she was thinking. Maybe she was secretly glad he wasn't just another run-of-the-mill sex maniac rock star. Maybe she'd actually enjoy a conversation for a change. But he rejected that idea. Strange women did not pick you up in a bar, paw at you in the back of a taxicab, and breathe hotly into your ear just to get you to talk about the best brands of guitar strings.

"It might help," Gary suggested, "if you knew how old I am. I mean, I have a deep voice for my age. People tend to think I'm older."

"Wait." She reached across him again and switched on a light. He squinted in the sudden brightness and saw that she was putting on glasses. He remembered that before they'd left the club she'd said something about the smoke irritating her contact lenses. Later she'd stumbled on the curb while trying to flag a cab. Could her vision be that bad? Now, with her glasses on, she stared at him in the light. "Oh, my God!" she gasped.

Gary winced. "I'll be eighteen in September."

Kathy lay back on her pillow and started to laugh. After a few moments she turned to him, her lips parted in a smile. "I almost broke the law," she said, and started to laugh again.

•

For a while they both lay on the bed, careful not to look at each other. Gary tried to imagine what Elvis Costello or Tom Petty would have done in this situation. It was obvious, wasn't it? Even Johnny Fantasy of the Zoomies would know what to do, and he was only a year or two older than Gary. But the Zoomies were a million miles ahead of the Electric Outlet. They even had their own single.

Kathy stirred beside him. It occurred to Gary that he just might want to get up and leave and spare them further embarrassment. Besides, the radio alarm clock on the night table said 6:45 and it took forever to get a bus back across town at that hour. Gary sat up. "I have to go now," he said.

"But it's not even seven," she said.

"My parents get worried if I'm not home by eight," he explained.

"In the morning?"

Gary shrugged. "It's a strange situation."

Two

Later, as Gary let himself into the brownstone on East Seventy-fourth Street, the familiar smell of cloves reached his nostrils. It was Eugenol, coming from the dentist's office on the first floor of the building. Gary could walk into any dentist's office that smelled of it and instantly feel at home, basically because this dentist's office *was* his home.

At the second-floor entrance he opened the door to his parents' apartment. It was a five-story brownstone town house and his parents lived on the two floors above the dental office. Gary's father was a dentist. So was Uncle Jack, his father's brother. Jack lived on the top two floors of the brownstone with his wife, Gary's Aunt Ruth, and his daughter, Gary's cousin Susan, who was also the bass player for the Electric Outlet. Even though she was a few months younger than Gary, Susan was living alone in the apartment upstairs while Jack and Ruth spent the year on a dental fellowship in Australia.

Inside, Gary took off his red high-top sneakers and walked carefully down the hall to his room, trying not to make any noise. But as he passed his parents' bedroom he could hear his mother mumbling. It was amazing—no matter how quiet he tried to be, she was always awake when he came in. Either she stayed up all night waiting or she slept so lightly that the turning of the key in the front door woke her.

Down the hall Gary eased open the door to the Shrine of the Rock-and-Roll Guitarist. It was his bedroom, actually, but he'd recently covered the walls with a layer of gray cardboard egg trays for soundproofing, and everywhere you looked there were posters and photos of rock and roll's great guitarists. This was a holy place. Gary's gods were guitarists from Hendrix and Clapton right down to Johnny Fantasy of the Zoomies. Guitarist worship was part of the rock-and-roll way of life. As far as Gary was concerned, there was no other way to live.

Outside, the sky above New York was blue and bright, but Gary was just getting undressed for bed. It was almost 8:00 A.M., and in a few minutes his parents would be getting up and his thirteen-year-old brother, Thomas, would be lacing his roller skates and turning on some noisy AM radio station full of plastic Top 40 hits. Gary pulled the shade down on his bedroom window and got into bed. He couldn't think of a better time to go to sleep.

.

He was up before dinner. His room reeked of cigarettes and sweat—smells he always brought home with him from the club—and down the hall he sought the sanctuary of a shower. But the bathroom door was locked and inside he could hear a hair dryer. Thomas was preparing himself for an evening of roller-skating.

"How long you gonna be?" Gary yelled through the door.

"Forever," came the reply.

Gary tightened his robe and continued down the hall. In the kitchen his father was sitting at the table, only his fingertips visible at the edges of *The New York Times*. As Gary sat down, Dr. Specter looked up briefly, as if to check the identity of this new companion, and then retreated again behind the paper. Standing near the stove, his mother smiled at him. But, as usual, Gary sensed that beneath her smile she was worried about something.

"Did it go all right last night?" she asked.

"Pretty good." Gary quickly gobbled down a roll and butter, and his mother smiled more comfortably. Her general rule of thumb was, no matter what her son did the night before, if he had an appetite the next day it couldn't have been too bad.

Across the table Dr. Specter lowered the newspaper until his shiny bald head and his eyes appeared. "Why does it suddenly smell like a bar in here?" he asked.

"Because your son works in a bar," Mrs. Specter answered.

Dr. Specter looked surprised. "You do?"

"Where do you think he's been every Friday and Saturday night for the last three months?" Gary's mother asked her husband.

"You're a bartender?" Dr. Specter asked, clearly confused.

"No, I play in a band," Gary said. "With Susan, remember?"

"Of course I remember," Dr. Specter said, sounding offended. "I just don't see why you have to come home smelling like that."

"Hazard of the profession," Gary said.

His father grumbled something and returned to the newspaper. Actually, Gary was surprised that his father had said anything about the way he smelled. Usually Dr. Specter's concern was focused only on that area between the chin and the nose known as the mouth. Anything that happened outside that area was irrelevant and therefore his wife's responsibility.

"For three months his son plays music in a bar until four in the morning and he doesn't notice," Gary's mother complained to no one in particular. Life was not fair to Mrs. Specter, as she was fond of telling anyone who would listen. She was stuck with a husband who knew from noth-

ing except molars and bicuspids. She had one son
who spent all his waking hours on roller skates
and another who was surely degenerating as a
result of playing rock-and-roll music in dark,
smoky bars. To hear her tell it, it was only a matter of time before Gary started living in rags in
the street, fishing his meals out of trash cans.

*Gary Specter and the First Step Toward Bum-
hood.*

Not that his mother didn't *try* to understand;
she tried but always failed. She worried about
everything: the people Gary mixed with at the
club, the drugs, the hours he kept, the homework
for school that he neglected to do, the lousy food
the club served, the possibility of a fire, shocks
from the electric guitar he played, diseases contracted by singing into a microphone some
stranger had just sung into, damage to his ear-
drums caused by the high volumes they played at,
getting mugged on the way home late at night. . . .
In her vision of the music world goblins and
demons lurked everywhere. She insisted she only
wanted Gary to be happy, which meant go to
college.

Actually, Gary had been accepted for the fall
semester at Bard College, but he doubted that he'd
go. The only reason he'd applied was because
Walter Becker and Donald Fagen of Steely Dan
had gone there. But Gary was wise enough to
know that simply going to Steely Dan's alma
mater didn't matter. Besides, none of the Zoomies

had gone to college. They'd graduated from high school and gone straight into the rock clubs. Just the other day at Julio's music shop Gary had heard someone say that the Zoomies were planning to tour with a big-name act in the fall. Gary imagined long black limousines, classy hotels, crowds of fans at stage doors, autograph hounds, groupies, photographers, interviewers, record contracts, Fame and Fortune. . . .

"*Gary, you're not listening!*" his mother yelled at him.

"What?" Gary said, startled.

"I was telling you that Susan didn't come home until seven this morning," Mrs. Specter said as she checked something in the oven. It smelled like chicken. Again.

"That was me," Gary told her.

"No, you came in at seven thirty-five," his mother replied. Maybe she slept with a stopwatch.

"Well, that's her business," Gary said.

"With her parents in Australia, it is also my business," his mother said.

"How come it bothers you more when she comes home late than when I do?" Gary asked.

His mother closed the oven door. "Because she could get into more trouble than you," she said.

"You mean get pregnant?"

Gary's mother appeared to shudder slightly. "No, dear, I just meant trouble. Nothing specific. You're a big strong boy and you can take care of yourself."

"Oh, you mean rape," Gary said.

Mrs. Specter rolled her eyes upward and shook her head.

Dinner was almost ready and Gary decided to make one last assault on the bathroom before he ate. "You know," he yelled through the door, "if you never leave the bathroom no one will be able to see how beautiful you really are."

"Aw, go listen to Bruce Springstone," came the reply.

"That's Spring*steen*," Gary yelled back.

"*Who cares?*" Thomas may have only been four years younger, but he was in another generation as far as music was concerned. "Born to disco," was inscribed on his favorite T-shirt. Gary sometimes wondered how they could possibly be related.

He banged his fist against the bathroom door. "Come on, you've been in there all day," he shouted. A moment later the bathroom door swung open and his brother, wearing tight blue jeans and a bright red sweat shirt, rolled out. Gary stared at his brother's feet. "You have to wear roller skates to the bathroom too?" he asked.

Thomas responded by making an obscene gesture with his arm and hand and then skating away down the hall. Gary sighed. There was a time when he would have clobbered his brother for showing such disrespect. Now it hardly seemed worth the effort. The kid was a lost cause.

Three

While Johnny Fantasy and the Zoomies were on their way to becoming famous rock stars, Gary Specter and the Electric Outlet labored each weekend in obscurity at a small rock-dance club on the Upper East Side called the Rock Garden. It was a new club—only the year before the building had been occupied by a Chinese restaurant with the same name—and it drew a steady drinking crowd of college students from New Jersey and Long Island. Gary suspected that Sleazy Larry, the club's owner, also let some local prostitutes join the crowd for the late show.

El Sleazo explained it to Gary this way: "If you wanna make it here, you got to get the early crowd thirsty and the late crowd horny." To the Outlet this meant playing a lot of fast dance numbers the first set and more slow stuff during the second. No big deal. In fact, the band liked the formula, because it let them get just about as low-down funky as they cared to get. And when it came to getting funky, the Electric Outlet made even the Zoomies look like a classical string quartet. Gary was certain that, given the chance, his band could become a top rock group. But when you only played in a place that still smelled like chop suey, it was hard to get discovered.

•

When Gary got to the Rock Garden that evening, the club was empty. It wouldn't start to fill up until nine, and the Electric Outlet wouldn't begin its first set until ten. Sleazy Larry was behind the bar. He was a creepy guy who wore dark suits and slicked his greasy hair down, like a gangster from the 1930s. But he was too small and wimpy to really frighten anyone. Gary watched while El Sleazo poured vodka from a nondescript bottle into an empty Smirnoff's bottle.

"These kids don't know the difference," Larry said when he noticed that Gary was watching him. "Besides, it all gets mixed with orange juice anyway."

Gary nodded. He knew Larry was in it only for the money. Not only did he refill brand-name bottles with inferior booze, but he watered down drinks and charged a buck and a half for sodas that were mostly ice. Even the band had to pay for its own drinks—at most other clubs the bands' drinks were on the house. Sleazy Larry was so cheap that when he bought the Rock Garden Chinese Restaurant to turn it into a rock club, he didn't even bother to change the name. He just tore down the "Chinese Restaurant" part of the sign and let the "Rock Garden" part stay, Chinese-style letters and all. People still came in once in a while to ask for a takeout order.

"Noticed you had some company when you left last night," Larry said, looking up from his vodka bottles and winking.

Gary just smiled back. It was funny the way people like Larry always wanted to believe that because Gary played guitar in a rock band he was a big stud. It fit their fantasies of what a rock star should be. Gary would have told him the truth about the previous night, but he already knew that Larry would prefer the fantasy. It was crazy, but it too was part of the act.

"Anyone here yet?" Gary asked.

El Sleazo nodded. "Yeah, your drummer's been in the men's room for fifteen minutes." He sounded disgusted.

Gary walked down past the small tables jammed so tightly together that he had to hold his breath to squeeze past them. He crossed the tiny dance floor and stage and headed for the john.

Ten feet from the door the air grew thick with marijuana smoke. Gary went in and found Karl, the Outlet's drummer, sitting on the toilet seat facing the door, staring blankly. If he saw Gary he made no sign of it. Gary stepped up to the urinal and took a whiz. Then he looked again through the haze of smoke at Karl and at the rest of the john. Even with the smoke, the Rock Garden's bathroom stank. It probably hadn't been cleaned in twenty years. How anyone could sit in it and get high was beyond him.

Karl stood up slowly. He was taller than Gary and thinner, and he had a terrible pimply complexion. Blown away on grass, wearing tattered, patched jeans and an old denim jacket, he looked like a cross between a hippie, a zombie, and a scarecrow. "Do you believe in life after birth?" he asked Gary solemnly.

Gary tried the hot tap in the sink, but no water came out. "Not as a rule," he answered.

Karl scratched his head. "My mother's coming tonight. I couldn't stop her."

"Don't knock it," Gary told him. "She could be the only fan we have." He was looking for paper towels, but he should have known better.

"Mothers can't be fans," Karl grumbled. "Once a mother, always a mother."

Gary finally had to wipe his hands on his jeans. The Rock Garden's bathroom was truly the Eighth Wonder of the World. No place could have been more disgusting. "Come on," he said, "let's do a sound check."

Outside they saw that Oscar, the Outlet's keyboard genius, had arrived and was setting up an ironing board on the stage. Karl and Gary stopped on the dance floor and watched curiously. Oscar was only a junior, but when he leaned over you could see that the hair on the top of his head was starting to thin. Even though he was a year younger than the rest of the band, he was a precocious musician, the son of a famous child prodigy pianist named Rudolf Roginoff, who had played at Carnegie Hall at fourteen, but had gone crazy before he was twenty. Oscar was born just before Rudolf became a certified nut case and had to be put away. Fortunately, the Roginoff family was wealthy. Unfortunately, Oscar sometimes seemed to be following in his father's mental footsteps.

After watching Oscar set up the ironing board, Karl pulled off his denim jacket and T-shirt and put them on it.

"What are you doing?" Oscar asked indignantly.

"I figured that if you were gonna do some ironing you could do my stuff too," Karl said.

Oscar threw the clothes back at Karl. Then he detached his electronic keyboard-synthesizer from its regular stand and, struggling under its weight, managed to lift it atop the ironing board. The board creaked and wobbled, but held up.

Gary watched this with interest. "Uh, Oscar," he said. "Is there any particular reason why you need to play on an ironing board?"

Oscar glared at him. Then again, Oscar glared at everyone. "Yes, there is," he replied.

"Might I ask what that reason is?" Gary said.

Oscar looked irately from Gary to Karl and back. "That," he said, "is a secret."

Four

At ten minutes of ten that night the Electric Outlet was waiting eagerly in the Rock Garden's dressing room for their cue to go out on stage and begin the first set. Thus far it had been a typical day for the band. Susan had not shown up for the sound check. Oscar had complained and delayed everything while he made minute adjustments in his electronic keyboard and the position of the ironing board. Then Karl got impatient and yelled at him. Then Oscar got angry and had a tantrum, screaming that the band was unprofessional and that the sound system at the Rock Garden was "beneath his artistic standards." That made Karl laugh, and Oscar stormed off the stage and out of the Rock Garden.

But now they were all together again in the dressing room. It seemed miraculous to Gary how playing rock and roll, even the anticipation of playing rock and roll, always changed Karl and

Oscar from weird, depressed crazies into eager, happy crazies. Almost every musician Gary knew was that way. Some were on the verge of being totally berserk except when they were playing rock. Rock was sanity, safer than Valium, more effective that seeing a shrink twice a week, and generally more fun than being committed to a mental institution. It was a kind of therapy. Rock-and-roll therapy. Gary had even written a song about it, the one the band always opened its sets with.

Just sitting in the Rock Garden's dressing room was enough to make anyone need a little Rock Therapy. The room was tiny and dim and creepy. You couldn't sit too close to the walls; cockroaches as big as Tootsie Rolls scurried around the peeling paint. Outside in the Rock Garden they could hear the crowd talking loudly over the taped music from the PA. Gary tried to make the minutes pass by wiping down the neck of his Fender Stratocaster. The guitar was a beauty—a 1965 red sunburst with custom Schaller tuning machines and a Schecter pickup assembly. It had cost Gary $450 and he'd installed the machines and pickups himself. Gary's mother said that if he loved his wife half as much as he loved that guitar she'd be a lucky woman.

Near him Karl sat on a wooden stool, enjoying a preperformance joint. Oscar, who'd already forgotten about his tantrum, was chatting with Susan, who'd managed to arrive just a few minutes before. Susan sat with the big Fender bass on her lap. Gary watched her.

"After 'Mama, Don't Cook No More Chicken for Me,'" Oscar was saying, "we ought to do 'I Fell in Love with the Baby-sitter.'"

Gary nodded and turned to his cousin. "You got the bass line for 'Baby-sitter' down?" he asked.

"Sure," Susan said. But Gary had his doubts. She'd messed it up the night before and had agreed to practice that day. Gary had been home all day and hadn't heard a thing from upstairs.

The set list was finished and the band got into their performing garb. Oscar always wore a black tuxedo with tails—the tux his father had worn during his classical concert performances. Karl changed from one T-shirt to another. Susan got into a short red chiffon dress with fishnet stockings and black spike heels. The dress was cut low in the front and she was wearing some kind of bra that made her breasts bulge up. She must have set her long, streaked blond hair because it curled and waved as it fell over her shoulders. The whole look was kind of a goof on styles from the 1960s, and Gary knew the crowd, especially the guys in the crowd, would love it.

Gary slipped on the straitjacket he'd bought in a costume store in Times Square. That night he was wearing it over a black T-shirt and jeans with red high-top sneakers for footwear. While Susan helped him tie the straitjacket loosely in the back, Karl told them that he'd heard a new Zoomies song on Evan Walker's all-night rock-and-roll radio show. "And they've got a big record display in the window of Bleecker Joe's record shop," he added.

News of the Zoomies' growing success always depressed Gary. Because the two bands were so close in age, he was constantly comparing the Outlet to them. Unfortunately, the Outlet rarely looked good in such comparisons. At the rate the Zoomies were going, it wouldn't be long before they signed an album contract with one of the big record companies like Arista or Warner. Gary couldn't imagine a company signing the Electric Outlet to an album contract. What would they call it—"Songs from a Former Chinese Restaurant"?

He looked around the dressing room, dejected. "And here we are stuck in this hole full of cockroaches."

"I think you're suffering from a Zoomie fixation," Susan told him.

"Yeah," Oscar concurred. "They're just a three-chord bubble-gum band."

"But professionally they're way ahead of us," Gary said. "You know how many great musicians are out on the streets driving cabs because they can't get their acts together? You have to be professional. You have to be organized. You gotta put out a single and have a manager to book dates at lots of clubs."

Karl had his drumsticks out and hit rat-a-tat rhythms on an old wooden chair. "You gotta have money, honey," he sang. "You need that bread, Fred. Must have the dough, Joe. Hey! Where's the moolah, Abdullah?"

Susan and Oscar laughed, but Gary wasn't amused. "You can laugh," he told them, "but I, for one, don't want to spend the rest of my life playing in this dump."

"No one said you were going to," Susan said.

"Why?" Gary asked. "You think a big record producer is just going to stroll in here one night looking for some egg rolls and discover us?"

"It happens," Karl said.

"In the movies, Karl," Gary told him.

Outside, the music had stopped and they could hear Sleazy Larry thanking everyone for coming to the Rock Garden. In the dressing room the Electric Outlet got up and stood by the door, waiting for their cue.

"And now, ladies and gentlemen"—Sleazy Larry was really hamming it up—"back for another headline performance at the Rock Garden, please welcome the Electric Outlet!"

There was some applause as the band ran out on the stage. As usual, when the crowd saw their outfits, especially Gary's straitjacket and Susan's sexy dress, there were laughs and catcalls. Meanwhile, the band got ready to play. Gary stood at the mike at the front of the stage, his arms still tied behind him in the straitjacket. The spotlight glared brightly into his eyes, making it hard for him to see. He turned his back to the crowd and checked the band. Oscar, Karl, and Susan nodded. Their amps were buzzing, the volume was turned up high.

Suddenly Gary jumped around. The band started with a roaring jolt, and Gary screamed:

> *"You know, they say I'm lazy,*
> *Don't want no responsibility.*
> *Just sit around the house all day*
> *Playin' songs from A to Z.*
> *Now the doctor thinks I'm crazy;*
> *He wants to use shock therapy,*
> *But I say, oh, no, doc, all I need's Rock*
> *Therapy!"*

Oscar and Karl sang the refrain:

> *"I need Rock, Rock, Rock Therapy,*
> *I need Rock, Rock, Rock Therapy."*

Meanwhile, Susan quickly undid the back of the straitjacket and Gary picked up his guitar and sang:

> *"Don't you hook up no electrodes to me.*
> *I need Rock, Rock, Rock Therapy."*

They rolled into the second verse:

> *"My daddy wanted to send me to a shrink*
> *So that he could analyze the way that I think*

But I said, Wait, it's just a little neurosee.
It'll clear right up with some Rock Therapy!"

By the time the Outlet started the second refrain people were dancing. Gary played the break while Oscar played rhythm on the electronic keyboard. Behind him Gary could feel the steady blasts of Karl's bass drum. Susan was kicking her legs like a cheerleader as she played the bass and half the guys in the audience had their eyes riveted to her. Everyone else was crowding onto the dance floor as waitresses struggled past them under trays filled with drinks.

Oscar took a short solo, and then it was time for Gary to sing again:

> *"Well, they told me to try this jacket on for*
> *size,*
> *And they shined all kinds of lights in my*
> *eyes.*
> *I can't understand why they'd take this*
> *guitar away from me.*
> *Don't they know about Rock Therapy?"*

Behind Gary the rest of the Outlet sang again: *"I need Rock, Rock, Rock Therapy . . ."* Gary was soaked with sweat. The dance floor was jammed with dancers, and the people sitting at the tables were clapping to the music. Gary felt supercharged—faster on guitar than a speeding Zoomie, more powerful than a thousand folk musicians, able to sing a hundred notes with a single breath! He danced, leaped, sailed across the stage, and sank to his knees, all the while squeezing impossible riffs out of the Stratocaster. Music coursed through his veins and he was once again transformed. Good-bye, high school student; hello, rock star.

Five

By 3:30 A.M. they were finished. Their agreement with Sleazy Larry was for four forty-minute sets separated by twenty-minute breaks, but somehow it never worked out that way. The sets were always longer and the breaks shorter. The band's problem was that they loved playing so much that they never wanted to quit.

In the dressing room the four band members caught their breath. Susan, Karl, and Gary drank beers and Oscar had 7-Up. They felt tired, but much too charged up from playing to go right home and go to sleep. Oscar again was the exception. Now that the music was over, he was his normal quarrelsome self, standing near the doorway sipping his soda and obviously impatient to get paid and go.

Gary suspected that Oscar was pissed. The Rock Garden's sound system had gone dead in the middle of the third set, leaving the band helpless and embarrassed on the stage while Sleazy Larry tried to fix it. And Susan's bass on "Baby-sitter" had been wrong again. It was frustrating—the band just wasn't going anywhere playing in a club like the Rock Garden and with a bass player who didn't know the songs, no matter how sexy she was on stage.

Gary reached into his pocket and pulled out the night's pay, crumpled handful of fives and tens that came to $80 minus whatever drinks the band had ordered. "I know what you're thinking, Oscar," he said as he divided up their money. "But I still say that until we find a better job somewhere else, a steady gig at the Rock Garden is better than no gig at all."

Oscar took his share of the night's earnings and didn't reply.

There was a knock on the dressing-room door and Gary opened it. Standing outside was Mrs. Roesch, Karl's mother. "Am I disturbing you?" she asked.

Gary glanced at Karl, who shrugged. He pulled the door open wider. "Of course not, Mrs. Roesch, come in." Like her son, Mrs. Roesch was tall and had red hair. Tonight she was wearing an old workshirt with a peace symbol embroidered on it, a pair of bell-bottom jeans that were too short, and thong sandals. An original member of the peace-and-love generation of the sixties, she'd even taken Karl to the Woodstock music festival when he was four years old. All Karl remembered of it was playing in the mud for four days.

"I thought you were terrific tonight," Mrs. Roesch said.

"Hey, thanks, Mrs. Roesch," Susan said.

"Yeah, we appreciate it," Gary said.

Mrs. Roesch turned to her son. "Karl, have you got anything to smoke?"

Karl made a face and reached into his shirt, pulling out a joint. "Geez, Mom, when are you going to start buying your own stuff?"

"When you start cooking your own dinners, washing your own laundry, and making your own bed," his mother replied. Mrs. Roesch and Karl lived together in a tiny one-bedroom apartment in Greenwich Village. The whereabouts of Mr. Roesch had been unclear for as long as Gary had known Karl.

Mrs. Roesch lit the joint, took a drag, and passed it around, but only Karl felt like smoking. Even though Karl had told them that his mother had taken dozens of acid trips, Gary still felt funny doing drugs around her. Maybe Karl was right. Once a mother, always a mother.

Oscar yawned; he wanted to go home. But first they had to agree on a day to practice after school during the coming week. Monday was no good because Karl had an appointment with the dermatologist. Mrs. Roesch didn't make much money, but she insisted that Karl go to a doctor for his pimples—one of the cardinal rules of rock and roll being that you couldn't get your picture on the cover of *Rolling Stone* with zits.

Tuesday was out because Susan had to work on a big design project for school. Wednesday Oscar and his mother were going to a concert at Carnegie Hall. "Look," Gary pleaded, "we have to practice. Most bands practice three or four times a week. How come we can't even do it once?" Much to his relief, everyone agreed to rehearse on Thursday.

Oscar turned and left without saying good-bye.

"What's with him?" Karl asked.

Gary shrugged. "How would you like to be sixteen and going bald?"

Karl scratched his head. "Probably beats the chronic zits."

"That's a great name for a band," Susan cracked.

Karl and his mother finished the joint and then Karl got up and said he was going to pack his drum set. Mrs. Roesch said she'd catch up with him in a moment, but after her son left the dressing room she closed the door and turned toward Gary.

"I'm sorry about the way Karl played tonight," she said, keeping her voice low so her son couldn't hear.

Gary was shocked. "I thought he was great."

"You're just being nice, I know," said Mrs. Roesch. "But if you only knew how hard he practices and how much he loves being in the band. I hope you're not thinking of getting a new drummer."

Gary looked at Susan and then at Mrs. Roesch. "Karl's my best friend," he said, amazed. "I'd never do that."

Mrs. Roesch smiled. "Thank you, Gary." She got up and went to help Karl pack up.

When she was gone, Gary turned to Susan and shook his head wearily. "I can't believe this," he said. "I've got a keyboard man who thinks he's too good for everyone. I've got a drummer with a mother who can't keep her nose out of the band's business. We're stuck in a club no one has ever heard of, playing for cockroaches, whores, and a bunch of college students who couldn't care less about the music as long as they can get drunk."

Susan got up and stood behind her cousin, massaging his tired shoulders. "We were good tonight, Gary," she said to soothe him.

"Yeah." He relaxed a little.

"Sometimes in the middle of the set," she said, "I close my eyes and pretend we're playing Madison Square Garden."

Gary laughed. "With our parents sitting in the front row."

Susan stopped massaging Gary's shoulders and reached behind her back to unzip the red dress. "Even if we play Madison Square Garden they won't be happy," she said. "Not unless it's a nine-to-five concert and you wear a tie."

Gary heard the long *zippp* as Susan undid her dress and started to pull the straps off her shoulders. A few moments passed while he listened to the rustling of clothes as Susan changed behind him. The only way out of this mess, he knew, was to produce their own single the way the Zoomies had. The better rock clubs didn't even pay attention to you until you had your own single. Once you had one, you could get some good gigs and maybe some people would notice you. Maybe you could get a few good reviews in the papers, cut a few more singles, and play some out-of-town clubs. Then you could develop a following like the Zoomies had and maybe get an offer to tour as an opening act for a big group. And finally, if everything went well and the band hung together, you might even get an album contract.

"Okay, you can look now," Susan said. Gary turned around to find her buttoning the front of a pink blouse. She had changed into tight green jeans and was closing her makeup bag as if she was getting ready to leave the dressing room.

"Uh, Susan?" Gary said, feeling nervous about what he had to say.

"Yes?"

"The bass on 'Baby-sitter' wasn't much better tonight."

Susan looked down and fidgeted a little with the strap of her bag. "I thought it sounded okay," she said.

"It was okay," Gary admitted, "but it could be

better. A lot better. Would you practice it this week? After school?"

Susan nodded and smiled at him, flashing very white, very straight teeth—Uncle Jack's pride and joy. "Yes, Cousin Gary," she said in a whiny voice to show that she thought he was being unreasonable. Then she left the room.

She doesn't take it seriously, Gary thought.

A few minutes later he had also changed out of his sweaty clothes and left the dressing room. The mood of the club was peaceful now; it was close to the 4:00 A.M. closing time. Two couples were dancing to some old fifties rhythm and blues and most of the tables were empty. Gary walked up to the bar. He was feeling tired, but he decided to stay and have one more beer before going home. After all, this was Saturday night, the big night out. What a joke. Maybe his mother was right about him and his guitar. The instrument had been his only steady Saturday night companion for the last two years.

He ordered a beer and looked around the club, noticing that Susan was sitting at one of the tables, jammed close to some guy Gary had never seen before. Gary felt a pang and tried to force it away. It was just another irony in his life that the only girl he was the least bit attracted to was his own cousin.

"Great show." Someone slapped him on the back. Gary turned around to say thanks, but the congratulator was already walking out the door. Gary turned back to his beer, feeling a little lonely, but not eager to go home. As long as he stayed at the Rock Garden, at least he was what he wanted to be—a rock musician. But as soon as he went home he would turn into his other self—a senior at Lenox Prep. Tomorrow he'd have to do homework and all week he'd be just another student in dumb classes.

Of course, it was April now; he wouldn't have to be a student for much longer. Once he graduated from high school he would be free. He didn't know what he would do to make money, but at least he'd finally be able to devote all his time to rock and roll. And maybe, if the band could somehow scrape together enough money to get a single out by the time he graduated, they'd have the whole summer to play the clubs. It sounded like paradise. With luck they might even catch up to the Zoomies by next fall.

Someone tapped him on the shoulder. "Got a second?" It was Sleazy Larry.

"Sure."

El Sleazo leaned against the bar beside him. He smelled of men's cologne and cigars. "Listen," the club owner said. "I got a couple of ideas I want to run by you, things I think could help your act."

Gary nodded.

Larry moved a little closer. "Now I think you got a great thing going for you, Gary," he said, rolling his little hand into a fist and tapping it lightly against the bar as he spoke. "But you got to make your act more accessible."

Gary looked at him. "How?"

"Well, start with your music," he said. "Every song you play is original. Now don't get me wrong—it's good music and the songs are entertaining. But people like to hear some familiar stuff too, you know? They want some songs they've heard on the radio, something they can feel comfortable with."

Gary restrained himself from pointing out that the crowd didn't exactly seem uncomfortable with the Electric Outlet's songs. "What were you thinking of?" he asked.

"Oh, maybe a little Led Zeppelin or some Blue Oyster Soup," Sleazy Larry said. "Whatever crap they're playing on the radio these days. I ain't saying give up your own music—just add to it." His knuckles rapped on the bar.

Gary took a sip of beer. "Anything else?"

"Well, to tell you the truth, Gary, I ain't crazy about the name of the band either," Larry said. "The Electric Outlet. I guess you meant it as wordplay. Like playing electric instruments is a kind of outlet for you, right?"

Gary shrugged.

"Frankly, Gary, it don't make it," Sleazy Larry said. "First of all, you should headline the group. You know, Gary Specter and the, uh, School Kids or something like that. You get me?"

Again Gary shrugged.

"Now, visually you're terrific," Larry continued. "I mean, that crazy kid jumping around in the tux and you in that straitjacket and, uh"—he paused and glanced at Gary, then spoke in a lower voice —"the girl, of course. She is one sexy little number. You could make better use of her."

Gary lifted an eyebrow. It was his cousin that El Sleazo was talking about. "You think so?"

The club owner grinned. "Sure, if you could get her to strut her stuff a little more. Know what I mean? Maybe show a little more skin. A band is like a developing country, Gary. You got to use your natural resources to their best advantage."

"Hmmm." *Gary Specter and the Third World Nations.*

"But your visual problem," Sleazy Larry continued, "is your drummer."

"How come?"

"Because he's an ugly kid with a bad case of acne and long dirty hair. The whole hippie look went out with the sixties, Gary. He turns people off." Larry moved his lips closer to Gary's ear. "And I don't like him smoking pot in the bathroom, either."

Gary stared down at his beer. Larry saw this and put his hand on his shoulder. Gary felt the little fingers kneading the muscles over his collarbone and gritted his teeth.

"Listen, Gary," Larry said softly. "I'm trying to do you a favor. I think you got tremendous potential, really. You're top-of-the-charts material. I just want to help you make it, okay?"

"I sure do appreciate that, Larry."

El Sleazo smiled. "So when you come back next weekend maybe you'll have taken some of my advice." As he said this, Larry reached down and gave Gary's rear end a light squeeze.

"Thanks, Larry," Gary said.

Sleazy Larry the club owner/rear end squeezer moved off to check the cash register receipts. It was a smart thing to do because if he'd made any more "friendly suggestions," Gary might have punched him in his sleazy nose. Gary got up and walked away from the bar, leaving his beer unfinished. *I'm trying to do you a favor.* Gary could have laughed. All El Sleazo was asking them to do was start playing Top 40 junk, have Susan do a striptease on stage, and get rid of Karl because the poor guy had a couple of zits. *I just want to help you make it.* Sure, sure, Larry, you just want us to help *you* make more bucks, you sleazeball.

Gary picked up his guitar case. There was only one problem. As much as he despised Sleazy Larry, the Rock Garden gig was the only thing the band had. And even a bad gig was better than no gig at all. He wondered if he should talk to Susan— certainly not about "strutting her stuff," but just about what they should do.

But when he looked toward the table where she

was sitting with her friend, whoever he was, the guy had one arm around her shoulders and was whispering in her ear. Gary turned away and left the club.

Six

"You are asking me to play 'Stairway to Heaven'?" Oscar yelled. He stormed around the study of his mother's Fifth Avenue apartment, nearly knocking over a large African warrior's shield made out of zebra skin that stood in one corner. "You actually think I would play 'Can't Get No Satisfaction'?" he ranted.

Gary sat in an overstuffed chair. He had come over after school to work on a new song with Oscar, who wrote all of the music for the band. He'd mentioned Larry's suggestion that they play some Top 40 stuff just to see what Oscar would think.

"Well, the answer is no, never! Forget it! I quit the band!"

Gary had his answer. He waited while Oscar stomped around some more. On his head Oscar was wearing something that looked like a light blue bathing cap. At the base of the cap was a small box with a dial from which a long electric cord ran to a socket in the wall. Gary noticed that as Oscar raved and stomped around the room he was careful not to stomp so far that he pulled the plug out of the wall. Each time Oscar passed, Gary got a whiff of something that smelled like hot tar just poured on a newly paved road.

"What is that thing on your head?" Gary asked.

"None of your business," Oscar yelled at him.

"Geez, Oscar," Gary said. "I was just asking. It's no big deal."

Oscar suddenly stopped and stared at him. "*No big deal?*" he screamed. "Maybe it's no big deal to you, but then again you're not going bald at the age of sixteen. You'll never know what it's like to be handicapped for the rest of your life." Oscar now glared up at the ceiling. "I curse whoever gave me these lousy genes!" he yelled.

"I think they're passed down from your maternal grandfather," Gary said.

"Damn you!" Oscar yelled upward, apparently at his maternal grandfather.

It was obvious to Gary that Oscar still had a few minutes of ranting and raving left, so he picked up an old magazine opened to an article about Oscar's family from a dusty pile next to the chair. Before Oscar's father came to America to be a famous child prodigy and go crazy, the Roginoffs had been an important Russian family. One of them had even been a prince. A little way down in the article, Gary found what he was looking for—Oscar's maternal grandfather had been Count Dmitri Fyodorovitch Marmeladov, but he was dead now.

"It won't do you any good," Gary said. "Your maternal grandfather is dead."

"I know he's dead, you jerk," Oscar snarled. Then to himself he said, "Why do I put up with these simpletons? Why am I in this band?" He placed his hand against his forehead. "Oh, God, I'm getting such a headache from this stupid thing." Then he lay down, stomach first, on a couch.

"Is that some kind of heat treatment?" Gary asked.

"No, it's electrostimulation," Oscar replied. "It's supposed to stimulate the scalp to grow more hair." He reached for a little glass bell at the foot of the couch and rang it. A moment later a small woman in a white maid's outfit appeared. "Aspirin," Oscar said. The woman nodded and left.

"What's that tar smell?" Gary asked.

"That's the conducting agent that carries the electricity from the cap to the scalp," Oscar replied, apparently subdued by the headache.

"You better disconnect it before you take a shower," Gary suggested.

Oscar rolled his eyes. "Thanks for the advice, Gary. I don't know how I've managed to survive without it." He paused for a moment, and then said, "Why do you aggravate me with stupid questions? Did you really think I'd play music by Black Sabbath?"

Gary shrugged. Actually, he was relieved, since he also hated the idea of playing another group's music.

Oscar looked at him. "Sometimes, Gary, I think that you don't understand my motivation for being part of the Electric Outlet. I see myself principally as a composer of contemporary music. I do not consider myself a performer. In fact, the only reason I perform is to make sure my music is played correctly. I have no interest whatsoever in playing another group's music. None."

When Oscar had first joined the Outlet, Gary had wondered what his reasons were. Until then, Oscar's musical tastes at Lenox Prep had been strictly classical and his attitude toward rock, New Wave, and punk had been condescending at best. In fact, the only rock pianist he'd ever heard of was Elton John, whom he said he detested. So Gary had been surprised when Oscar answered the ad for a keyboard man that he'd put up on the school bulletin board. Now he knew better. Oscar was a closet rock-and-roller. He still wouldn't admit that he was a performer, but if you saw one of the Outlet's sets you'd quickly realize that Oscar, more than anyone in the band, strove to put on a good show. Oddly enough, Oscar's antics on stage reminded Gary of Elton John.

The maid reappeared carrying a small platter

on which lay two aspirins. Oscar looked down at the two white tablets and then back at the woman. "Thank you," he said, speaking through clenched teeth. "Now, would you be so kind as to bring me some water?"

The woman nodded. She seemed embarrassed by her omission and started to leave.

"Oh, Claire?" Oscar said.

The woman stopped.

"Make sure it's in a glass."

Gary wondered how Oscar had avoided being murdered thus far in his life. In some ways he was the most immature member of the group. You had to remember, after all, that he was only a junior. Gary also happened to know that Oscar's mother still bought his clothes for him and sometimes even laid them out so that Oscar would know what to wear to school in the morning. Oscar had also told Gary that he had gone to a Camp Running Creek for two summers. One day, reading through the *Times* magazine's camp section, Gary had seen the camp advertised—it specialized in bed wetters.

But in other ways, especially the way he acted toward adults and teachers, he seemed more fearless than the others. When Oscar got mad, even Gary stayed out of his way. Teachers at Lenox Prep called him Oscar the Terrible.

Claire returned with a glass of water, which Oscar accepted silently. Working with Oscar was difficult. Living with him must have been impossible. Oscar never liked the lyrics Gary wrote and the only way Gary could get him to compose music was to promise that he'd improve the words later. Somehow this never got done, but Oscar didn't seem to notice.

Gary read Oscar some lyrics to a new song called "Educated Fool." "What do you think?" he asked when he'd finished.

Oscar pushed himself up from the couch, took the page of lyrics, and walked to the grand piano in the den, pulling his electric cord behind him. "The lyrics are infantile," Oscar said, toying with the piano keys with one hand. While Gary watched, Oscar mumbled the words and doodled with the piano. He tried them one way, then another, then another. Ten minutes later he played Gary the refrain, half an hour later he had the verse. Then he got up, saying his head still hurt. "I'll figure out a beginning and end later," he groaned, lying down on the couch again.

Gary nodded. Despite Oscar's craziness, when it came to music, he was unreal.

Seven

The Electric Outlet played at the Rock Garden every weekend during April. They did not add songs by Led Zeppelin to their repertoire, nor did Karl leave the band. And if Susan strutted her stuff any more or less, it was strictly of her own accord and not a result of a suggestion from Sleazy Larry, Gary, or anyone else.

Several suggestions of new names for the band were considered, since this was the only one of Sleazy Larry's suggestions that Gary told them all about. He discovered that no one else in the band was crazy about the Electric Outlet either, so each member was asked to come up with something new. Susan suggested they call themselves the Young and the Restless. Oscar suggested the Over-achievers. Gary wanted the Neurotics, and Karl actually liked the Chronic Zits. But no one liked anyone else's suggestions, so the Electric Outlet remained the Electric Outlet until further notice.

Gary thought their shows at the Rock Garden went well. The club was crowded every Friday and Saturday night—not bursting at the seams, but the tables were full of drinkers for the early show and droolers for the late. People danced and had a good time. Gary thought he recognized faces in the crowd that returned from weekend to weekend. El Sleazo didn't offer his suggestions again, and since business continued to be good, Gary assumed he'd thought better of them.

The Friday night of the first weekend in May, after Gary had waited for Susan to get home from school, they carried their amplifiers down the stairs of the brownstone and out to the street. Both amps rolled on casters and they pushed them the several blocks to the Rock Garden.

When they got there, Karl was outside sitting on the cymbal box of his drum set, slouched over a smoking cigarette.

"How come you're not inside?" Gary asked.

Karl shrugged and pointed toward a dirty white van parked at the curb. As they watched, a burly guy with a long black ponytail came out of the van carrying a bass drum. He was wearing a black T-shirt with the words Cosmic Charlie stenciled on it in white letters. He carried the drum right past Gary and into the club.

"What's going on?" Gary asked, looking back

at the van. It had Cosmic Charlie stenciled on it too.

"They say they're playing tonight," Karl said.

Susan frowned. Gary looked at the Rock Garden's front door. "Is Larry in there?" he asked.

Karl shook his head. "Just that guy Joe who sets up the bar. He says he doesn't know anything about it."

Gary left his amp on the sidewalk and went into the club. On the way he passed the glass showcase that announced each night's act. Under "Appearing Tonight" was a picture of four hairy musicians, one of whom was the guy Gary had just seen in the van. The announcement read: "Appearing for the first time at the Rock Garden, New Jersey's foremost Grateful Dead band, COSMIC CHARLIE, playing all the Dead's greatest songs and more."

Gary stepped into the Rock Garden. He felt like Sheriff Matt Dillon stepping through the swinging doors of the Lone Star Saloon for a showdown. Up on the stage the four Cosmic Charlies were setting up their equipment. There was no mistaking them. Every piece of equipment—the drums, amps, keyboards, monitors—had Cosmic Charlie stenciled on it. Even the Cosmic Charlies had their name stenciled on them. Maybe they just had a hard time remembering who they were.

Gary stopped at the edge of the stage. "Didn't Larry tell you guys another band was supposed to play here tonight?" he asked. The Cosmic Charlies ignored him and Gary got mad. It was one thing to be ignored by famous musicians, but quite another to be ignored by a bunch of Dead clones from Piscataway. "You better clear that equipment off the stage," he said. "Because we're the regular weekend band here."

One of the Charlies pulled a folded piece of paper from his shirt pocket and tossed it toward him. Gary unfolded the paper. It was a copy of a contract specifying that the Charlies were to play that night and the next—four forty-minute sets with twenty-minute breaks in between—at a price of $250 for the two nights. Gary refolded the contract and handed it back. He was dumbstruck.

On the way out of the Rock Garden, he stopped by the bar and spoke to Joe, the part-time bartender. "What time's Larry coming tonight?" he asked.

"He said he'd be late," Joe answered, hardly looking up from the limes he was slicing.

"How late?" Gary asked.

Joe shrugged. Gary could tell he knew and just didn't want to say. "I don't know—just late."

Gary was disgusted. He went back outside.

"What's going on?" Susan asked him.

"Sleazy Larry signed those guys to play tonight," Gary said, his stomach twisting around inside him. "They've got a contract and everything."

Karl shook his head in disbelief. "Why would he do that?"

Gary stared at the entrance to the Rock Garden.

He knew exactly why Sleazy Larry had done it. Because Karl was still in the band and because they weren't playing songs by Blue Oyster Cult and because Susan wasn't doing a striptease on stage every set. Gary could feel his heart pounding. What a bastard that Larry was. Not even telling them they were fired. No wonder he was afraid to come down to the club that afternoon. Gary turned back to Susan and Karl. There was nothing any of them could do now. "We might as well forget it," he told them. "Let's go home." Then he went down to a pay phone on the corner to call Oscar and tell him not to come. Oscar, the great composer who "hated" performing, sounded crushed. He even asked Gary if the band wanted to rehearse that night just so that they would have a chance to play together, but Gary was in no mood for rehearsing.

Gary hung up the phone and turned around to see Karl arguing with one of the Cosmic Charlies. Susan had one of Karl's arms and was trying to pull him away from the husky Charlie, who was clenching and unclenching his fists angrily. Gary ran toward them.

"What are ya gonna do about it, huh? . . . huh?" The Charlie was snarling at Karl as Gary got in between them. He pushed Karl back and turned to the Charlie.

"Look, why don't you just leave him alone and go play your stupid gig," Gary shouted.

With Gary and Karl there, the Charlie didn't seem so eager to fight and turned away. When he was gone Gary asked what had happened. "He made a crack," Susan said. "He wanted to know why I was hanging around with a bunch of high school wimps."

Karl was still seething. "You should've let me at him, Gary. I would have murdered him." Gary just sighed. Considering that Karl was built like an emaciated giraffe, while the Cosmic Charlie looked like a well-fed gorilla, he had doubts about who'd be murdering whom.

Meanwhile, Susan sat down on her bass amp, looking sad. Gary was still angry. The band had played hard and well, filled the Rock Garden, and sold a lot of drinks. No one had complained about their original songs or even requested any songs by other groups. And Sleazy Larry didn't even have the balls to tell them they were canned. Gary's stomach was churning and his head pounded. It was completely, utterly, totally unjust.

Suddenly there was a loud crash and Gary and Susan both jumped. Behind them the Rock Garden's showcase had dissolved into a heap of broken glass as a piece of brick sailed through it. Gary turned around and saw Karl brushing some dirt from his hands. He was smiling.

A second later Joe rushed out of the club. "I know who you are," he yelled at Karl. "I'm telling Larry!"

Gary's first impulse was to shake Karl's hand. Susan stood up and yelled back at Joe, "You do that, and while you're at it, you can tell him he's a sleazy little worm, too."

Eight

That evening, Gary's mother had two unexpected dinner guests. "Why aren't you at the club?" she asked Susan and Gary, who sat together glumly at the dining room table. Gary winced. He knew if he told his mother what had happened she'd find something in it to worry about—maybe that the police were going to come and arrest him as an accomplice to a showcase breaking. Or maybe because he had probably incurred the wrath of all the Deadheads in Piscataway, New Jersey.

Dr. Specter, of course, didn't even realize that his son and niece weren't supposed to be at dinner. He was trying to tell a joke. Gary's father had never told a joke right in his life, but occasionally, when moved by blind inspiration, he tried. "A fellow came in the office this morning for a prophylaxis and asked for laughing gas," he began.

"I thought you got prophylactics in a drugstore, Uncle Harold," Susan said, grinning slyly.

Dr. Specter momentarily lost his voice.

"No, Susan," said Gary's mother. "A prophylaxis is a form of cleaning teeth. A prophylactic is . . ."

"Uh, Mom," Gary interrupted her. "I think Susan knows what a prophylactic is."

Gary's mother frowned. "Well, excuse me for being so naïve," she said defensively, and got up and went into the kitchen.

Dr. Specter found his voice again. "Well, as I was saying, this fellow wanted laughing gas just to have his teeth cleaned. So I told him that's not painless dentistry, that's brainless dentistry!" He paused, waiting for them to laugh. But Susan only groaned and Gary rolled his eyes. When his father tried to tell a joke it was like an anesthetic —you either went numb or fell asleep. Susan called him Audio Sominex.

A medium-length, blow-dried razor cut cruised smoothly through the kitchen and into the dining room—Gary's brother, Thomas, who lately insisted that everyone call him Tony.

"What have I told you about roller skates in the house?" Dr. Specter said sternly.

"I forget," Thomas replied.

"Thomas," Mrs. Specter called from the kitchen. "You know you're not to wear them at the dinner table."

"Aw, Mom," Thomas moaned, "everyone else does."

"Who is everyone else?" Gary asked.

"Take a flying leap." Thomas sneered at his brother.

"Thomas!" Mrs. Specter yelled. No one was sure what Thomas meant, but everyone was certain that Thomas knew it wasn't the kind of thing you were supposed to say at the dinner table.

"Call me Tony," Thomas yelled back. He sat down next to Susan, who leaned over and kissed him on the cheek.

"Hi, little cuz," she said affectionately, ruffling his hair as if he were a pet dog.

In an instant Thomas burst from his chair, almost knocking Susan over. "My hair!" he screamed, rolling backwards on his skates and delicately touching the displaced strands with his fingers. "I can't believe you did that, you dumb dink!" And with a roar of polyurethane wheels on the wooden floor of the hallway he disappeared into the hair repair center, otherwise known as the bathroom.

"What's a dink?" asked Susan.

Gary shrugged.

Mrs. Specter returned from the kitchen and they started dinner. Chicken as usual. Six out of seven nights his mother made chicken. No wonder Susan stayed out as many nights as she could.

"Gary," his mother said as they ate, "we had a

very interesting visitor in the office today." His mother often filled in at the office when one of the regular assistants was out sick or on vacation.

"Aw, Mom, do we always have to talk about the office?" Gary asked. It seemed like the only thing his parents could talk about at dinner was cavities and bridgework. It was as predictable as the chicken.

Mrs. Specter raised an eyebrow. "This might interest you, Gary."

"Let me guess," Gary said, "you had the world's foremost authority on napkin holders." Susan giggled. Gary's mother was always telling them about "interesting" patients who turned out to be the most boring people you ever heard of. Together, she and his father were Mr. and Mrs. Audio Sominex.

"No," Mrs. Specter said. "In fact, this young man is a rock-and-roll musician."

Now Gary looked at his mother, but he didn't say a thing.

Mrs. Specter smiled. "His name is Barry Fine and he plays with a group called, uh . . ."

"Sold Out," Gary said, amazed. Sold Out was one of rock's premier show bands, in New York that week to play five nights at Madison Square Garden. Gary couldn't believe it. "Here? In Dad's office!?"

Mrs. Specter nodded.

"How?" Gary asked.

"He was recommended by one of Uncle Jack's patients who's in the entertainment business."

"I can't believe it," Gary moaned. There in his house, Barry Fine!

Now Dr. Specter looked up from his chicken. "Why, is he famous or something?"

"Are you kidding?" Gary said. "If they made a recording of that guy's farts it would go double platinum."

His mother tried to look offended, but then she giggled.

"What did he need?" Gary asked.

"Nothing," Dr. Specter said. "Just a loose cap. I glued it and he was gone."

"Caps?" Gary said.

"All the way back to the molars," said his father. "Or, I should say, to where the molars were."

"Were?"

"Had 'em all pulled," his father said. "Nothing but gum after the last bicuspid. He'll be sorry someday."

"Models sometimes do that to thin down their faces," Susan said.

"He had his molars pulled to thin down his face?" Gary asked, poking his cheeks with his fingers.

Mrs. Specter looked at him. "Don't get any ideas, Gary."

Gary didn't like the thought of having all those teeth pulled anyway.

"He was a very nice man," Mrs. Specter said. "I told him about you and asked if he had any advice."

"What did he say?" Gary asked.

"He said that every week a dozen teenaged boys and girls ask him the same questions and he tells them all to go to college and enjoy music as a hobby, not a career," his mother said.

"I get the message, Mom."

But his mother had more messages. "You might also be interested in learning how old Mr. Fine is."

Gary and Susan exchanged glances. Sold Out had been big for about three years. If, Gary figured, it had taken them another three years before that to make it and you added a couple of years of just banging around, that came to eight years. The latest he would have started was eighteen or twenty years old, so Gary figured around twenty-eight. Susan guessed twenty-six.

"Thirty-six," Mrs. Specter said. "And he told me their group first started playing together twelve years ago."

"Twelve years?" Gary said, surprised. That represented more than two-thirds of his life span so far.

"With this band," his mother said. "He played with two other bands before that."

"Well, some bands make it faster," Gary said.

"And some bands don't make it at all." This came from the lips of Thomas (also known as Tony) Specter, who had just rolled in from the bathroom complete with repaired hair. "Especially bands who call themselves the Electric Outlet."

"We're working on a new name," Gary said.

"Gary and the Dorks," Thomas suggested.

"You better shut up or I'll mess your hair."

"Enough, boys," said Dr. Specter, a living monument to parental authority.

"Did you hear someone?" Thomas a.k.a. Tony asked.

"Thomas!" his mother snapped sternly.

"It's Tony!"

And so on.

•

After dinner Thomas rolled off to meet his friends for the early session at the local roller rink. Dr. Specter sat back in his chair and flossed his teeth. When Gary was younger, his father had gone to the bathroom after dinner to floss, but now he just sat at the table, running the string between his teeth and wiping whatever gook got caught on it into his napkin. It was a pretty disgusting habit, but they'd long since given up telling him so.

Susan got up and quickly helped Gary's mother clear the dishes from the table. It was obvious that she was in a rush to go back upstairs. When the last of the dishes had been cleared, Susan thanked her aunt for dinner and started to leave the room.

"You're going out?" Gary's mother asked.

Susan nodded. "Uh-huh."

"You won't be back too late, I hope," Mrs. Specter said.

Susan stopped. "Mom said on weekends I can come in when I want, Aunt Liz. She said she'd trust my judgment."

Gary's mother flushed. "It's not that I don't trust your judgment, dear, but you're my responsibility while your parents are away. Think of the position I'd be in if something should happen to you."

Susan pushed her blond hair back over her shoulder. "I promise nothing will happen to me," she said with a forced smile, and then left the room.

Mrs. Specter turned to her son. "Do you know where she's going?"

Gary shook his head.

"Would you find out for me?"

Gary sat up. "Aw, Mom, it's none of our business. Aunt Ruth said . . ."

His mother had on her life's-been-cruel-to-me look.

"Aw, come on, Mom—that's not fair," Gary complained.

His mother put on her life-hasn't-been-fair-to-me-either look. Gary knew he was going to lose this battle. If he didn't find out where Susan was going, it would be just another in the long line of disappointments in his mother's life. Considering that she already had a senior space cadet for a husband, one son who wore roller skates to bed, and another who aspired to be a musical bum, perhaps she had had enough disappointments for now.

The door to Uncle Jack's apartment upstairs was locked, so Gary rang the bell. No one answered and he rang again. A few moments later he heard Susan's voice asking who it was.

"Paul McCartney," Gary said. "Come on, Susan, open up."

The door opened and Susan was standing there, wearing a red terry-cloth bathrobe, a white towel wrapped around her head. "I thought so," she said.

Gary stepped into the apartment. "I've been sent to find out where you're going tonight," he confessed.

Susan nodded, turned, and walked back down the hall. "I'll tell you in a second. Just let me dry my hair."

Gary sat down on a couch in the living room. He liked this apartment much more than his parents' apartment. Aunt Ruth's was airier and brighter. The floors were whitewashed and the rooms were well lit with track lighting. His parents' apartment was dark and cluttered with heavy wooden furniture and dusty rugs. It was no surprise that the décors of the two apartments reflected the general dispositions of the two families. His, downstairs, was earthly and burdened; Susan's was ethereal and free.

"Want to come up to my room?" Susan yelled from upstairs.

"Uh, I'll wait for you down here," Gary yelled back.

But a moment later Susan appeared in the hallway. "For God's sake, Gary," she said, "don't be a silly."

Gary rose and reluctantly followed her. Susan's room was in the back and up the stairs on the top floor. It wasn't very large or sunny and, as Gary noticed when he stepped into it, it was an unbelievable mess—clothes, records, and books strewn all over the bed, floor, and desk. Gary remembered that the last time he'd been in the room it could have won a Good Housekeeping award for juvenile neatness. But that was before Susan's parents had gone to Australia.

Susan pulled some underwear off the chair and sat down at the vanity mirror to blow dry her hair. "I'm only going to the Bottom Line with Michael," she yelled over the noise of the dryer. The Bottom Line was one of the biggest and most famous rock clubs in the city. Normally you had to buy tickets weeks in advance to get in.

"That's pretty fast," Gary yelled back, referring to the fact that until a few hours before, they'd planned to play at the Rock Garden that night. "Who's Michael and how'd he get tickets?"

"Michael is an associate publicity director for Columbia Records and he always has tickets," Susan shouted.

Gary was shocked. "At Columbia Records? What a connection! Susan, how come you haven't invited him to hear us?"

His cousin shook her head. "No one takes high school bands seriously, Gary. Michael says they break up when everyone goes to college."

"Well, tell him we're not going to college," Gary yelled.

"*I* might," Susan yelled back. She'd been accepted at the Rhode Island School of Design, where the Talking Heads had gone.

"Not if we're doing well," Gary shouted. "You said you'd take a year off if things looked promising."

Susan nodded, but not exactly with enthusiasm.

"If this guy's an associate publicity director, he must be pretty old," Gary yelled.

"Twenty-seven."

Gary whistled and sang a bar from an old Lovin' Spoonful song, "*A younger girl keeps rollin' 'cross my mind.*" But he wasn't really surprised. Susan had always acted older than other girls her age. It wasn't just that she'd used makeup or had worn a bra earlier—nor was she really beautiful or blessed with a fantastic body. Instead, there was something about her self-assurance and friendliness that always struck Gary as being beyond her years. She didn't frighten guys away by being defensive or catty and she rarely did anything that Gary would call immature. She seemed to make guys feel confident and relaxed. In junior high she'd dated guys in high school, and in high school she'd gone out with college-aged men. Still, going out with a twenty-seven-year-old was some kind of record for her.

"You didn't exactly run away from that older woman a few weeks ago," Susan observed.

That caught Gary by surprise. He didn't think anyone besides Sleazy Larry had seen him leave the Rock Garden that night with Kathy. "Uh, well, that was different."

"Why?"

Gary saw that the only way he'd be able to explain that one was by confessing the miserable truth. "We didn't do anything."

Susan laughed. "And, my dear cousin, your mother's concern is that I really might 'do something,' is that it?"

"Geez, Susan, you're only seventeen."

"So are you."

"Yeah," Gary stammered. "But I act like it."

Susan smiled and then turned off the hair dryer and sat down on the bed next to him. She put her arm around his shoulders and gave him a friendly hug. Gary could smell his cousin's freshly washed skin and hair, and he could feel her breasts through the robe against his arm. And inside himself he could feel that urge, that gravity, as if Susan were the earth and he was falling toward her. It made him remember the crush he'd had on her all the years they were growing up together.

Once, when he was too young to know better,

he'd told his mother he wanted to marry Susan when they grew up. But his mother had told him that it wouldn't be allowed.

"How come?" he'd asked.

"Because there'd be a problem with your recessive genes," she said.

He was ten at the time—what did he know about recessive genes? But it was the message he remembered: You will not marry your first cousin who was brought up more like a sister to you.

Still, a year later, at age eleven, they had kissed. First, it was just an experiment. But later, well, there were some pretty heavy make-out sessions. They grew closer together, were practically inseparable in school and out, were best friends, confidants, and . . . secretly more.

One day, when they were twelve, Susan had said that since their last names were both Specter, they could run away and everyone would think they were married. Even Gary was realistic enough to know that two twelve-year-old newlyweds checking into a motel would raise a few eyebrows. But when their parents were out they pretended they were married. Gary had insisted to himself that they didn't know any better, even long after he knew they did.

When two families live one on top of the other, certain things do not go unnoticed. Sixth grade was ending, nothing truly alarming had happened, but Aunt Ruth thought it was a good idea if Gary and Susan went to separate junior high schools.

Again the message was clear. So Gary was enrolled at Lenox Prep, a private school, and Susan continued in public school, waiting to go to the city High School of Art and Design. They made different friends and even had a few outside crushes, but after dinner they always did their homework together.

Then, one freezing cold winter night during their thirteenth year, with both sets of parents out and nothing good on television, Gary discovered where his aunt and uncle kept their liquor. Susan and Gary tried a few drinks and got giddy. It was so cold in the house that night that they decided to get a blanket and put it over them on the living room couch. Then they tried another drink and got still giddier. There was some fooling around under the blanket. It started to get a little hot under the blanket and a few pieces of clothes were discarded. Some underwear was pulled askew and then, suddenly and without any warning, there was a stain on the blanket.

Victims of uncontrollable teenaged lust! Even now Gary remembered how startled Susan was when his body had suddenly arched upward and the blanket got sort of damp and sticky. Later, in the laundry room, she had cried as she put the blanket through the washing machine. Gary had tried to help, but she yelled that she never wanted to see him again. He felt terrible.

After that night, Susan and Gary avoided each other. Nearly two years passed before they could sit comfortably in the same room, and another year passed before they did anything together. Then, in eleventh grade, they had the idea for the band, and Susan asked Gary to teach her the bass. Slowly they became friends again, although it seemed to Gary that part of that friendship was based on the understanding that they wouldn't talk about what had happened that cold winter night when they were younger.

And yet, Gary still sometimes caught himself wondering. After all, she was still the only girl he knew whom he sincerely felt attracted to. Was it *that* impossible?

In his cousin's room, Gary shook the thought from his mind. He must have been crazy to think there was any hope for a relationship between them. *Gary Specter and the Impossible Dream.*

"I better get dressed or I'll be late," Susan said, getting up.

Gary could tell that she had suddenly become uncomfortable with him being in her bedroom too. But before he left he said, "I know I have no right to say this, Susan, but please be careful tonight. I mean, I think you're a great person, but you gotta wonder what a twenty-seven-year-old publicity director for a record company wants with a seventeen-year-old girl."

Gary was afraid Susan would get mad at him for saying that, but instead she only said, "I know what he wants, Gary. You don't have to play amateur psychiatrist with me."

"Well, is it worth a free ticket to the Bottom Line and a ride in the company limo?" he asked.

"I haven't gotten any other offers."

"What about some of the guys from school?" Geez, he sounded just like his mother.

Susan smiled wryly. "They never ask me out because they all think I go out with older men. Besides, there's no difference between them and Michael except that we'd probably wind up at Nathan's playing electronic space games instead of at the Bottom Line. After the show they all have the same idea."

"Well, I guess I just thought it would be easier to say no to someone your own age," Gary said.

Susan laughed and kissed him on the cheek before steering him toward the door. "You really do think like a seventeen-year-old sometimes, Gary," she said, but not without affection.

Nine

Back downstairs Gary learned from his mother that Karl had called. He called him back.

"You wanna go to a party?" Karl asked. "My mom's going to this one in SoHo and she says we should come. I told her about what that bastard Larry did and I guess she wants to cheer us up." Karl's mother worked for a gay clothing designer and most of her friends were gay men, so Gary had a pretty good idea of what the party was going to be like. Karl said his mother liked gay men because they weren't sexually threatening to her. Everyone was an amateur psychiatrist.

"I don't know, Karl," Gary said. He was still pretty bummed out about losing the gig at the Rock Garden. "It's a weird scene down there."

"She says this'll be pretty straight. There may even be some music people there. Come on, Gary, don't mope around the house all night because of that jerk Larry."

Gary wasn't convinced, but he didn't have anything better to do. Used to be when he felt really down he could go to Nathan's and play electronic space games for a couple of hours. But after what Susan said that night he even felt funny about doing that. "I'll meet you down there," he told Karl. "But I'm not promising I'll stay."

"Okay." Karl gave him an address on Prince Street.

Gary hung up, turned around, and almost bumped into his mother. "What are you doing, eavesdropping?" he asked.

"If it's a 'weird scene down there,' " his mother said, "why are you going?" His mother was suspicious of Karl's mother because: a) she was the mother of Karl; b) she was divorced; c) she hung around with gay men; and d) she hadn't put up a fight when Karl dropped out of Lenox Prep. Karl said they didn't have money for him to go to college and all his mother wanted him to do was be a rock drummer anyway. It seemed reasonable to Gary, but completely unreasonable to Mrs. Specter. Gary sometimes wondered how his mother survived in the modern age.

"Don't give me a hard time tonight," Gary told her. "I'm just going down there to look. If it's too freaky I'll probably leave."

"If it's too freaky they may not let you leave," Mrs. Specter replied. Gary gave his mother an exasperated look and she switched to a different tack. "Wouldn't you like to go out with a nice girl instead?"

Gary eyed his mother suspiciously. "And I'll bet you've already got her picked out," he said.

"One of your father's patients, Mrs. Vayle, has a daughter your age studying at Juilliard. She says she cannot tear the girl away from her studies. Since you are both interested in music, I thought that you and she might, er, have something in common."

"What instrument does she play?" Gary asked.

"Well, uh, I think Mrs. Vayle said she plays the tuba."

Gary rolled his eyes. "You want me to go out with a girl who plays the tuba?"

"Well," his mother said, "I don't see what difference—"

Gary just shook his head and didn't explain. What could you say to a mother who wanted you to go out with a girl who played the tuba?

Since it was a party, Gary put on a vest over his T-shirt and wore his old leather bomber jacket. He took the subway downtown. Subways and buses were usually good places to do some heavy thinking, because you wanted to block out the noise and odors and graffiti and weirdos. But tonight he wished he couldn't think. At least, not about losing the first steady gig the band had ever had, and not about Susan. He wished he'd never asked about whom she would be with tonight. He could just picture this Michael dude—long hair and a droopy mustache and a red baseball jacket with *Columbia Records* in big white letters on the back. Gary had seen his type before at the Bottom Line and the other big clubs. Tonight he'd show Susan off to his friends and on Monday morning he'd be sitting with his $200 cowboy boots up on his desk, sipping coffee, and smirking while he told the guys in the office about his little groupie. Gary felt his teeth grind. He wished he could punch the guy out. *Gary Specter and the Avengers.*

At the Spring Street stop he climbed out of the subway station. Two very tall women wearing tight black pants and high heels passed him and one of them winked. Gary suddenly realized they were guys in drag. This city is weird, he thought.

Prince Street was dark and lined with tall old buildings that had once been factories, but had been turned into lofts and studios by artists. As Gary walked along he noticed that most of the floors above him were lit and hanging plants adorned the windows. At one corner he paused and peered into a small restaurant. On the street outside, chauffeurs waited in long black limousines—like the limos famous rock stars got driven around in. Inside the restaurant, men in ties and jackets and women in long dresses dined by candlelight. It seems like a strange place for such a fancy restaurant, Gary thought as he continued on. He'd seen no rock stars inside.

At the address Karl had given him, Gary went inside and started climbing some old, creaky wooden steps. He was already certain he'd only stay a few minutes and then leave. Partying was the last thing he wanted to do that night, but at least it would make the time go until the next day, when he would take a handful of taped cassettes of the Electric Outlet's best songs and start making the rounds of the rock clubs looking for new gigs. The hallway at the top of the stairs was dark and smoky. Gary could hear music inside. He rang the doorbell.

The door opened and a torrent of music, noise, and marijuana smoke rushed into the hall. A neatly dressed man with short blond hair, wearing a navy alligator shirt and pressed khaki pants, held out his hand.

Gary shook it. "Hi, I'm—"

"Oh, yes." The man cut him short. "I'm sure you're somebody and somebody told you about this party, so come in and enjoy yourself. My name is Phil and I'm the host, in case you can't tell. If you want a drink, the bar is that way." Phil pointed to his right. "Or, if you prefer chemical stimulants, just follow the music."

And before Gary could even react, the doorbell was ringing again and Phil was busy repeating his message to the next guest.

As far as Gary could see, almost everyone at the party was considerably older than he. But that didn't bother him as much as it once had, thanks to the examples Oscar and Susan set. He'd recently begun to realize that older people were often as scared of him as he was of them. He decided to get a beer and headed for the kitchen.

No sooner had he gotten there than Karl appeared beside him. "Hey, man, you made it."

"Yeah." Gary pulled a can of beer out of a plastic garbage pail filled with ice and cans.

"Nice place, huh?" Karl asked.

Gary looked around. There were a lot of plants and even some small trees around the loft. He looked up and saw that the whole ceiling was one large skylight. There were lots of modern-looking couches and chairs, too. "Yeah, nice," he said. "The guy who lives here doesn't seem like, uh, what I expected."

Karl nodded. "Phil's a lawyer for ABC Records."

"Why would a lawyer live in a loft?" Gary asked. "I thought they were for artists."

"My old lady says artists can't afford the rents anymore," Karl said. "Everyone down here now is either a banker, a lawyer, or just plain rich. It's pretty good if you work on Wall Street." Karl himself worked on Wall Street—as a messenger.

"What does a lawyer need this much space for?" Gary asked.

Karl shrugged. "A big ego, maybe."

Gary looked around at the crowd. They were pretty conservatively dressed, but there were a couple of standouts, like the woman who was wearing only a lacy pink slip and the man dressed in a long purple robe and carrying a large, colorful parrot on his shoulder. On a couch near them two people were lifting tiny spoonfuls of white powder to their noses from a miniature silver clamshell. "Coke," Karl whispered.

They went into the large room where everyone was dancing. On the way they passed an attractive dark-haired women wearing tight white slacks and a white vest with no blouse or bra under it. Gary could see a lot and what he couldn't see was easy to imagine.

"Wow, did you see that?" Karl gasped after they'd passed her.

Gary nodded. He was surprised Karl had mentioned her. Karl rarely talked about girls. Susan, an amateur psychiatrist in her own right, said Karl repressed his feelings about girls because of something that must have happened between his own mother and father when he was a kid. Gary just figured Karl's acne turned girls off.

"She wasn't any older than us," Karl said.

"Oh, come on, sure she was," Gary said. Not that he'd taken such a good look at her *face*, but no girls their age were confident enough to wear an outfit like that—not even Susan.

"I'm telling you," Karl said, looking back at her. "She was."

"Well, go introduce yourself," Gary said.

Karl laughed disdainfully. "Are you kidding? I walk down Broadway and even the prostitutes won't proposition me."

For a while they stood against the wall watching people dance. Someone had turned the lights down and it was hard to see the faces of the dancers, but every once in a while Karl would point out his mother, dancing with one of her friends.

Gary finished a beer and decided to go back to the kitchen and get another one. "You want one?" he asked Karl.

"No," Karl said. "I dropped a 'lude before."

"A Quaalude?" Gary asked, surprised. Karl nodded slowly. "Does your mom know?" Gary asked.

Karl grinned. "What do you mean, does she know? She gave it to me. It's a real mellow drug. She says it keeps me out of trouble."

Gary glanced at his friend in wonder and then went to get another beer. He couldn't imagine being stoned on Quaaludes in the same room with his parents; just the sight of them was enough to send you on a bad trip. On his way to the kitchen he caught the eye of the girl in the white vest. Gary smiled at her and kept going.

Karl was smoking a cigarette when Gary returned. For a while they stood against the wall and listened to the music. Gary sipped his beer; Karl took deep drags off the butt and exhaled slowly.

"Hey, how's Lenox Prep?" Karl asked.

Gary shrugged. "Same old drag. Good thing it's gonna be over after next month."

"Yeah." Karl nodded in the shadows. "But at least you'll graduate," he said wistfully.

"Yeah, so?"

"Well, I mean, what if the Electric Outlet doesn't make it?" Karl asked. "What do I do? I'm just a high school dropout. I gotta go back down to Wall Street and be a messenger for the rest of my life."

"Karl," Gary said, "you're a good drummer. Even if the Electric Outlet doesn't make it, you'd keep drumming."

Karl slouched against the wall. "I dunno. Sometimes I think my mother wants me to be a rock star drummer more than I do," he said. "If the Electric Outlet broke up, I don't know what I'd do. I don't even know any other bands to get into."

Gary started to say something, but then he stopped. It had never occurred to him that the members of the band were really depending on him to make it. Sure, he wanted the Electric Outlet to succeed, but even if it didn't he knew he'd find work playing guitar with some group, somewhere. It was weird to think that Karl would be lost without the Electric Outlet. It sort of put a lot of responsibility on Gary's shoulders. A lot more than he wanted.

Out of the crowd, Gary recognized Karl's mother coming toward them, leading someone by the hand. Mrs. Roesch was wearing green Army fatigues and a peasant blouse and looked pretty cute. The guy she was dragging behind her had short black hair and a short black goatee beard. He looked older than Mrs. Roesch and was wearing a black turtleneck sweater and a black jacket.

"Hello, Gary," Karl's mother said. "I want you and Karl to meet Evan Walker."

"You're Evan Walker?" Karl nearly shouted. Gary could understand his friend's excitement. Walker's all-night rock-and-roll show was the best thing on the radio.

The man in black nodded. He didn't look happy.

"I told Evan about your band," Karl's mother said. "He said he'd love to hear you."

"But not right now," Evan Walker said, looking around as if for an escape route.

"You mean you want to come to one of our gigs?" Karl asked. Gary felt like kicking him in the leg to remind him they didn't have any gigs anymore.

"Well, I'm awfully busy," Evan Walker said. "Perhaps you could send me a single."

"We don't have a record," Karl said. "But if we had one made, do you think you'd play it?" The Quaaludes seemed to numb whatever sense of tact he normally had.

"Well, perhaps, if it's good," Evan Walker said in a tone that implied that he seriously doubted that it would be.

"It will be," Gary said. Evan Walker now looked at Gary for the first time.

"And you have to have some kind of distribution," Evan Walker said. "I can't play a single just because you've talked your local record shop into carrying five copies. You've got to have distribution behind you so the kids who hear it can get it."

"We will," Gary said.

Evan Walker smiled and nodded impatiently. "That's great," he said insincerely, and started moving away, even though Karl's mother still had a firm grip on his arm. "Wait, Evan," she yelled gaily as the man in black dragged her back into the crowd of dancers.

"Wow, Gary, he said he'd play our single." Karl was ecstatic.

"If it's good and if we can get it distributed," Gary said.

"Oh, you can do that, Gary," Karl said. That was another thing about Karl and the other members of the band. They believed that Gary could make it all happen. It was like they needed to believe that or else there was no reason to go through all the crap they went through to play. But Gary had no idea how to get a record distributed—other than to stand on the observation deck of the Empire State Building and fling records like Frisbees out into the air. That would distribute them all right.

Just then the girl in the white vest walked past them. Karl, in his stoned gleefulness, called out to her. "Hey, see this guy," he pointed at Gary.

"He's gonna be the greatest rock star in the world someday."

The girl stopped and looked skeptically at Gary.

"And I'm his drummer," Karl added.

"Are you *really* a musician?" the girl asked. Karl was right—she didn't look much older than they.

"Yeah." Gary kind of smiled and pushed some hair out of his eyes.

The girl smiled back and Gary noticed she had nice teeth. Family habit, noticing teeth. "What do you play?" she asked.

"He plays guitar and sings," Karl said.

"Hmm," the girl said. She was looking at Gary as if she couldn't decide whether to believe him or not.

"And, uh, what do you do?" Gary asked.

"Oh, me." She smiled enticingly. "I'm a secretary, but I do anything."

Ten

Now that the Electric Outlet had no steady gig, they had to practice twice a week or more. Since none of their parents had the room or could stand the volume the band played at, they rented a rehearsal studio on 52nd Street for two or three hours after school or on the weekend. The rehearsal studio was just a big room with a stage at one end and it cost twelve bucks an hour, which the band split four ways. With no gig money coming in, Gary was spending most of his weekly allowance on rehearsal time.

No sooner had everyone arrived for rehearsal than Karl started telling Susan and Oscar about the girl in the white vest. "I couldn't believe it," he told them. "Gary asked her what she did and she said, 'I'm a secretary but I'll do anything you want.'"

Susan and Oscar both looked at Gary, who was

standing near a big black Vox amp, tuning his guitar.

"Then what happened?" Oscar asked eagerly.

Karl glanced at Gary.

"We danced a couple of dances," Gary said. "And then I got bored and went home."

"Really?" Oscar was disappointed.

"Can you believe it?" Karl said. "She even came over to me after he left and asked if there was something wrong with him."

"And what did you say?" Susan asked.

Karl looked sheepish. "I said I wasn't sure about Gary, but there was nothing wrong with me."

"Then what happened?" Oscar asked.

Karl shrugged. "She said she suddenly wasn't feeling well."

Susan patted his shoulder sympathetically.

"Aw, it didn't bother me," Karl said. "She wasn't my type anyway."

Gary and Oscar had finished "Educated Fool" over the weekend and they wanted to play it for the rest of the band. First, Oscar got everyone in the mood with some fancy flourishes he had cooked up for the beginning of the song. Then Gary sang:

> *"Hey, baby, I can show you a swell time.*
> *Just grab a pencil and fill in this line.*
> *Who gets the highest grades and best SAT*
> *scores*

But'll probably spend his life sweepin'
up floors?"

"Who?" Susan yelled out.

"Me!" Gary pointed to himself. " *'Cause I'm an*
educated fool."

Oscar played rhythm on the keyboard and sang
the refrain. *"Yes, he's an educated fool."*

Gary sang:

> *"Well, I'm hot stuff in school,*
> *But I can't tell squat from cool—*
> *Must be an educated fool."*

Karl was able to pick up the drum beat pretty
quickly and Susan tried to fill in the bass line
as Gary started the second verse:

> *"Well, I'm always the class valedictorian,*
> *On the honor society, and school historian,*
> *Yes, I could read before I was three.*
> *So how come everyone always talks down*
> *to me?"*

Oscar: " *'Cause you're an educated fool."*

Gary: *"Yes, I'm an educated fool.*
> *Well, I get straight A's*
> *But I forget the days.*
> *Must be an educated fool."*

Gary took a guitar break and then went into the third verse:

> *"Well, science and math, literature, too—*
> *I can do them all much better than you.*
> *I'll take the honors—you can have the rest.*
> *But in the exam of life I'll probably*
> *flunk the test."*

Oscar groaned. "We'll have to work on that line some more," he said as the band kept playing.

> Gary: *"Well, I got the brownest nose."*
> Oscar: *"And the ugliest clothes."*
> Gary: *"Must be an educated fool."*
> Oscar: *"Yes, he's an educated fool."*

The song ended. Gary watched the band members' faces for reactions. Susan was smiling. He knew she'd like it. "Karl, what do you think?"

Karl whacked his snare drum. "Good song!"

Gary turned to Oscar, the toughest critic. "How did it sound?"

"Needs work," Oscar said. That was his highest rating.

"What would you say if we made it the flip side of 'Rock Therapy' on our single?" Gary asked.

No one seemed to have any objections. Gary smiled. "Well, then, I guess we better learn it pretty quickly, because we're gonna take it into the studio this weekend."

"*What?*" they all said at once.

"I said"—Gary whipped up a crescendo of chords on his guitar for dramatic effect—"we are recording this weekend at Cat's Eye Studios on West Forty-fourth Street from 2:00 A.M. until 5:00 A.M. Sunday morning. I have already booked us."

He was immediately hit by a barrage of questions. "How come?" "Why so soon?" "Who's gonna pay for it?"

Gary raised his hands. "I shall explain. First, we are recording now because I spent all day Saturday walking around to clubs and dropping off tapes of our songs, and most of the club managers I talked to said they'd take us more seriously if we could show them a single. It's the only way to go if you really want to make it. In other words, fellow Outlets, it's inevitable. We must record.

"Second. On Friday night, at a party Karl so inaccurately described mainly because his sense of perception was, shall we say, chemically altered"—Gary winked at Karl—"we were introduced to Mr. Evan Walker, the late-night disc jockey at WHAT. Now, I wouldn't say that Mr. Walker gave us much encouragement, but I believe he might play our single."

"What about money for the recording session and for pressing the record?" Susan asked.

"Well, the band's general fund has enough money for Cat's Eye's special Sunday morning off-hours forty-five-dollar recording rate."

Oscar frowned. "What do they record with? Mattel toy tape recorders or something?"

"They've got an eight-track," Gary said. "That's all we need."

"And what about pressing the single?" Karl asked.

"They press the record for us," Gary said. "The minimum order is five hundred copies, and they'll make a label and a record jacket too."

"How much?" Susan asked.

"They said they could even recommend some distributors who would listen to it," Gary said.

"How much?" asked Karl.

"And even if we can't get distributors, we can take it to record stores ourselves and ask them to stock it," Gary said.

"How much?" Oscar asked.

"And if the four of us each take a few copies to the radio—"

Oscar hit his electronic keyboard with the volume way up. The small rehearsal room shook with music so thick it almost felt liquid as Oscar roared into something that sounded like Beethoven's Funky Fifth. After a few moments he stopped. Gary's ears rang in the stunning silence that followed.

"All we're asking," Oscar said calmly, "is, how much?"

"Nine hundred and fifty dollars."

Karl flicked a drumstick and a cymbal crashed. "Pocket change," he said.

"Don't be cute," Susan said morosely.

"I know it's a lot of money," Gary said, "but if we divide it up four ways, it's only two hundred thirty-seven fifty apiece. If worse comes to worst, we can borrow it from our parents."

Susan looked from Gary to Oscar to Karl. "I think worse is definitely going to come to worst."

Eleven

The Electric Outlet arrived at Cat's Eye Studios at 1:30 A.M. Sunday morning. Over near Eleventh Avenue, West 44th Street was a pretty creepy area, and at that time of night it was at its creepiest. The studio was located in a squat gray building that looked like a garage with no windows. Gary knew there was no sense in having windows in that neighborhood unless you got some weird enjoyment out of having them smashed every week.

The only working streetlight on the block lit the sidewalk just in front of the studio, and they saw that the ground was covered with broken glass, bottle tops, and other garbage. A bum was sprawled unconscious against a wall near them. As Gary and the band unloaded their equipment from the taxis that had brought them to the studio, police sirens wailed constantly in the dark distance. Gary felt nervous, and he was sure the other members of the band felt the same, if not worse. As the last cab pulled away from the curb, Karl suddenly let out a yell that made them all jump.

"What's wrong?"

"Did you see that?" Karl's voice quivered. He pointed at a dark iron storm sewer in the street.

"What?"

"A rat the size of a football," Karl said. "I swear, it ran right over my foot."

"Oh, God," Oscar groaned.

Gary banged on the flat gray metal door of the studio. The rest of the band huddled silently with their equipment in the light of the streetlamp, watching the ground for giant rats. No one answered the door and Gary knocked again.

"Maybe there's a night bell," Susan said.

Gary found a button next to the doorframe and pressed it. Still no answer. He looked up and down West 44th Street. It was empty and dark. Most of the buildings were abandoned or boarded up. Way down at the end of the block cars and cabs passed, going up Tenth Avenue. If they had to get a cab it would be an incredible drag, literally, to haul all their equipment down there. And there was always the possibility that they might get mugged on the way, or even attacked by *a whole pack* of giant rats.

Gary pressed the button again. They could hear the buzzer ringing insistently inside, but when he let go there was nothing but silence.

"Oh, crap," Karl said anxiously. "First the Rock Garden, now this."

Susan and Oscar looked at Gary. "We might as well wait a while," Gary told them. "Maybe they're recording and can't hear us."

"We'd hear them," Karl said.

"Well," Gary said, "maybe they went to the bathroom."

"Right," Oscar said sourly. "The whole place goes to the bathroom at the same time."

"All right, give me a break," Gary snapped back. He left the door and stood with the rest of the band under the streetlight. Everyone was tense. Here they were, stuck in a sleazy part of town in the middle of the night—four teenagers and about three thousand dollars worth of musical equipment.

"The longer we wait here, the more likely some street gang will come along and rob us," Oscar complained.

"We can't leave yet," Gary argued. "It's not even two."

"If they're not here now, what makes you think they're going to be here at two?" Oscar asked anxiously. Gary could see that the kid was really scared.

"Hey, cool it, Oscar," Karl said.

Oscar turned on him and shouted, *"Don't tell me to cool it, you ignorant jerk!"*

"Oscar, please calm down," Susan begged.

"Listen." Gary spoke quickly, trying to get their

minds off the present predicament. "Has everyone managed to get together the money for the record?"

"I think I can get it," Susan said. Gary knew she'd spoken long distance to her parents in Australia that week. They'd probably agreed to lend her the money.

"I have it," Oscar said.

"Good," Gary said. He planned to take his share out of his savings account. Asking his mother and father for a loan to make a single would be like pulling teeth without Novocain.

"I can only get about a hundred bucks," Karl said. He took a joint out of his pocket and lit it.

"You're the only one of us who has a job," Oscar said irritably.

"Yeah," Karl said, "but I made this deal with my mom that if I wasn't gonna go to school I'd help pay the rent and stuff." He took a long toke off the joint and offered it around, but no one was in the mood.

"Maybe if you'd spent a little less money on pot," Oscar suggested snidely.

Karl took a quick step toward the keyboard player and clenched his fist. "Shut up or I'll break your face, you little creep."

Oscar quickly jumped away. "That's right," he yelled back at Karl. "Pick on someone who's half your size, a year younger, and going bald."

Gary grabbed Karl by the arm. "We're gonna go look for a phone," he told everyone. "I'll try to

call inside, and if no one answers, we'll go home."
He pulled Karl down the dark street with him.
"Hurry up," Susan called out as they left.

As they walked down the street looking for a
phone booth, Karl complained about Oscar. He
was right that Oscar was an obnoxious, con-
ceited pain, but Gary knew Oscar was just as right
about Karl's spending so much money on grass
that he didn't have enough for his share of the
single. There was nothing Gary could do, as usual.
He couldn't take sides—not if he wanted to keep
the band together.

They approached Tenth Avenue. So far all
they'd seen were abandoned buildings and lots
filled with rubble. As they reached the corner,
Gary saw a woman wearing a long blond wig and
tight red hot pants leaning against the wall.

"You boys want a date?" she asked seductively.

"Uh, no thanks," Gary said, walking quickly
in the opposite direction. Karl followed. "Well,"
Gary said to him, "you finally got propositioned."

"Must be so dark out she can't see my zits," Karl
mumbled. They found a phone booth. Shattered
heaps of glass that had once been its windows
lay on the ground around it. Gary picked up the
receiver and put a dime in the slot.

"Hey, look," Karl said before Gary started dial-
ing. The cord to the receiver dangled loosely in
the air where it had been severed from the
phone.

Gary flicked the coin return lever, but the phone wouldn't give his dime back. "Damn," he grumbled. That was his only dime. Karl didn't have any change either.

"You want to ask her for change?" Karl asked, nodding toward the prostitute, who was still watching them.

"Forget it." Gary left the booth and they started back toward the studio. The whole thing was a bust. Gary was so disgusted and mad he felt like smashing something, but everything around him was already smashed. What a bummer, he thought. Who needed this business anyway? Maybe Barry Fine, the thirty-six-year-old lead guitarist for Sold Out, was right after all. Maybe he should go to college and become a dentist and play in a band on weekends as a hobby. He could call the band *The Cavities* or maybe *Gary Specter and the Bite Plates*. At least he wouldn't have to risk his life trying to record a single no one was ever going to listen to anyway.

"Hey, look!" Karl yelled. Down the street they saw the silhouette of a large man approaching Oscar and Susan in front of the studio. Gary quickly broke into a sprint, with Karl right behind him. Ahead he could see Oscar and Susan in the streetlight, backing away from their equipment as the man got closer to them. Gary ran faster. He could see now that the guy was lifting up a guitar case.

"Leave that alone!" Gary screamed. He would fight to the death for that Stratocaster. The man quickly put the guitar case down. At the same time he turned and stared at Gary, who stopped just a few feet away.

"What's buggin' you, huh?" the man asked indignantly. He was dressed in a pair of designer jeans and a white V-neck sweater. Around his neck were several gold chains. He didn't exactly fit Gary's image of a mugger.

Gary glanced at Susan and Oscar. They too looked surprised, but not scared, and Gary was too out of breath to ask what was going on. A second later Karl stopped beside him, panting. The man in the white sweater took a key from his pocket and opened the door of the studio. Then he turned and said to Gary, "Carry 'em yourself. I don't care." He went inside and turned on some lights.

Karl nudged Gary; he was grinning. But Gary shook his head. "For a second there," he said, "I thought it was all over."

Oscar nodded. "You looked really scared."

"And you weren't?" Karl asked.

Oscar laughed haughtily. "Not for a second."

The man's name was Walter and he was the night sound engineer for Cat's Eye Studios. When Gary explained why he'd yelled at him, Walter laughed and said, "Can't say that I blame you." Then he said that the studio hadn't had any recording time booked from 10:00 P.M. to 2:00 A.M.

that night, so he'd locked up and gone out for a drink. Gary noticed that the engineer had a gold star in one of his front teeth.

"But where's everyone else?" Karl asked, looking around at the empty studio.

"No one else but me," Walter said. "What do you expect for forty-five dollars an hour?"

At one end of the studio was a small glass-enclosed control booth with speakers hanging by chains from the ceiling. From inside it, Walter spoke to them through a microphone while he adjusted lots of knobs and checked sound levels. All this took a while and Gary could feel the band growing impatient to play. They could hardly keep their hands off their instruments and a couple of times they even started playing short riffs until Walter ordered them to stop.

Finally the engineer had them run through each song and gave them some advice. "Listen, drummer," he said through the mike, after they'd played "Rock Therapy." "Go easier on the cymbals in the beginning and then pour it on at the end. And bass player, you have to fill in more notes on the breaks to get that good funky sound." Even Oscar listened when Walter told him when to add his background vocals. Gary was amazed. In his mind he'd always had an idea of how the songs should sound, but they never quite sounded that way when the band played them. Now it was as if Walter was reading his mind and telling them exactly what to do to make the songs perfect.

Walter had them play the songs over and over until they sounded flawless. Meanwhile, Gary was getting more impatient. He really appreciated Walter's taking the time to make sure they all got it right, but not only was this costing them money—everyone was also starting to get a little bored. By Gary's count they'd already played "Rock Therapy" twelve times and "Educated Fool" nine times.

And Walter still wanted to check the levels!

Gary waved at him through the window. "Can we record now?"

"Record what?" Walter asked through the mike.

"Come on, Walter," Gary yelled at the control booth. "We only have enough money for three hours of studio time."

In the control booth Walter looked up at the clock on the wall behind him. "Well, then, you might as well pack up your stuff," he said.

"*What?*" The band yelled in unison.

"Because," Walter continued, "I got it all right here on tape. And there's nothing left for you to do." The engineer had a big smile on his face.

"I don't get it," said Karl.

"We're finished," Gary told him. "He recorded us and we didn't even know it."

" 'Cause if you had," Walter said over the mike, "you would have choked up and missed enough notes to keep us here until next week."

Then the engineer invited the band into the control booth and played the master tapes of their songs for them. Gary, Susan, Oscar, and Karl stood around the big sound board, mesmerized, as "Rock Therapy" cascaded out of the control booth speakers at them. From the expression on their faces Gary could tell that no one really believed that the tight, professional-sounding song thumping out of the speakers was actually theirs.

"Was that really us?" Susan squealed after both songs were played.

Karl was shaking his head in disbelief. "Incredible, man, just incredible."

Even Oscar said, "I didn't think we sounded that good."

Gary turned to Walter. "What do you think?"

"I think you've got a long road ahead," Walter said solemnly.

The broad smiles on everybody's faces quickly disappeared. "But," Walter added, the gold star in his tooth sparkling in the studio light, "you're the first band I've heard in months that's even on that road. Most of the bands I record here are so lost they don't even know where the road begins."

Gary and the rest of the band looked at each other, not sure whether to be happy, unhappy, or what. Walter must have read the expressions on their faces, because he said, "Hey, that's nothing to get depressed about. Like I said, you're on your way. That's more than you can say for most bands your age."

"But you said we still have a long way to go," Karl said glumly.

"Sure," Walter replied. "But remember, even the Beatles had a long way to go once."

Half an hour later the band had packed up its equipment and was waiting on the sidewalk outside the studio for the cabs Walter had called to take them home. It was after 5:00 A.M., the sky was getting light, and everyone was exhausted. Sitting on his keyboard case, Oscar could hardly keep his eyes open. The cabs arrived and Walter locked up the studio and helped them load the amps and drum set in.

Finally Oscar and Karl were gone, and Susan was waiting in the last cab for Gary, who stood on the sidewalk with Walter.

"I'll let you know as soon as I have all the money together," Gary said. Walter nodded. Gary knew the studio wouldn't do anything about converting the tapes they had just made into a record until they were paid in full. "Just one last question," Gary said. "What can we do to be better?"

The sound engineer glanced toward the cab as if to make sure Susan couldn't hear. "Your bassist is weak," he said quietly. "On the tapes I could mix it down some, but it'll show in a live performance. She's got talent, but she needs to develop technique."

Gary nodded. The news wasn't surprising. "Anything else?"

Walter shook his head. "Just exposure, man. Practice and exposure and luck." Then he reached into his pocket and pulled out a bright orange business card that said, WALTER SLOVES, ENGINEER FOR THE BEST SOUNDS AROUND.

"Next time you record," Walter said. "Call me."

Gary shook his hand. "You bet."

Twelve

Memorial Day was approaching and the band was still short of the money they needed to press the single—basically because Karl couldn't put up his full share. After paying his own share, Gary had nothing left in savings, and Susan said she couldn't ask her parents for more. They asked Oscar if he would lend the money to Karl, but he refused "on principle."

More than three weeks had passed since Gary dropped off cassette tapes of the band's songs at various rock clubs around the city. Since then he'd called each club twice to see if the owners had listened to them. The answers were depressingly alike: "I got two hundred cassettes here. Which one was you?" or "I haven't had time to listen yet. Maybe next month" or "Yeah, you're good, but so are the other hundred bands that want to play here."

One owner of a small brand-new club called Galaxy One way downtown near the financial district said that he could let the band play an audition night in July.

"July?" Gary said. "That's three months from now."

"We're not really gonna be open until June," the owner said. "And I can't pay, either."

"Not even expenses?"

"Nope."

But Gary accepted the date anyway. It was the only offer he'd had. Sometimes he found himself wishing the Electric Outlet still played for Sleazy Larry. Seeing how hard it was to get gigs at other clubs made him realize how lucky they'd been to have a steady job—even at a dump like the Rock Garden.

•

Sitting with Susan on a bench in a playground near their house one afternoon after school, Gary confessed to his cousin that he was worried the band would break up if they didn't get another gig soon. Susan was manicuring her nails and squinting as smoke from a cigarette lodged between her lips rose to her eyes.

"Don't worry, something will come up," she said, pausing from her nails to take the cigarette out of her lips.

Gary gazed across the playground at a bunch of guys playing basketball. "I don't know, Susan.

Sometimes things just don't happen like that. Sometimes you have to *make* them happen. If you just sit around and wait, you could wait forever."

Susan inhaled on the cigarette and started to cough.

"When did you start smoking?" Gary asked.

"I just have one once in a while," Susan replied irritably, dabbing her eyes with the sleeve of her blouse.

Gary fidgeted a little on the hard wooden bench. He'd originally sat down with Susan to talk to her about her bass playing, but it wasn't easy. He had to be delicate, not giving her the impression that she was a bad bass player, but simply one who needed to work harder.

"Been practicing much?" he asked finally.

Susan crushed out the cigarette. "You're not being very subtle, dear cousin," she teased him.

"Well, remember I told you that 'Baby-sitter' needed some work," Gary said cautiously.

"I know, I know," Susan replied. "I just wish I had more time."

Gary suspected that Susan's recent lack of time was somehow linked to her new boyfriend, Michael, the publicity guy. Not that she actually had a lot of dates with him. On the weekends they went out either on Friday or Saturday night and maybe she saw him once or twice during the week, but she usually had to be in early for school the next day. Still, Michael seemed to take up a lot of Susan's time even when she wasn't with him, whether it was time she spent talking about him on the phone with friends, or the time she spent waiting for him to call, or the time she just spent thinking about him. Whatever it was, Gary had noticed that Susan just didn't seem as interested in the band as she once had. And it showed in her playing. Recently Oscar had even suggested they look for a new bass player.

"Maybe we could go over it together," Gary said.

Susan sighed. "Gary, I wish I could spend four hours a day practicing like you, I really do. But there are other things on my mind." She picked up her cuticle scissors, but then put them down again as if she'd had a new thought. "Gary, haven't you ever gotten sidetracked from music?" she asked. "By a girl or something?"

Gary shrugged. He almost wished it would happen.

"Well, I have," Susan said. "Sometimes even something in school will get me excited and I'll forget about music and just want to concentrate on it. That never happens to you?"

Gary thought about it. At school he was taking a poetry-writing seminar because it was the closest thing they offered to songwriting. And he was taking music history, which was kind of interesting because he got to read about how all those old famous guys like Bach and Mozart had made it. Then there was geometry, physics, and U.S. history. He spent most of his time in those courses daydreaming about stuff like what the cover of the Electric Outlet's first album would look like, and what he'd say the day *Rolling Stone* interviewed him, and what it would be like when they did their first big concert with a group like Blondie and he got to hang out backstage with Debbie Harry and her band. No, nothing in school really excited him—certainly not enough to make him forget about music.

"But what if you *can't be* a rock star?" Susan asked.

What would he do then? Gary tried to imagine it, but all he got was a blank. Life without rock and roll hardly seemed worth it. Well, maybe if he tried really hard to think about it he could imagine himself being an astronaut. Not really an astronaut as much as a space explorer—captain of an interplanetary cruise ship hopping from galaxy to galaxy. "I could probably get into space," Gary told his cousin. "Like flying around between planets and solar systems."

Susan smiled. "That's very realistic of you, Gary."

Just then a small, teenaged body clad in tight jeans and a T-shirt glided gracefully through the entrance on the other side of the playground. Gary and Susan watched as the body cut across the basketball court, disrupting the game in progress and drawing angry shouts from the players. A second later Tony a.k.a. Thomas Specter skidded to a halt in front of Gary and Susan.

"You know," Gary warned him, "someday you're gonna get your head kicked in."

"By who?" asked Thomas as he carefully combed back a lock of hair that had come loose as he skated.

"By whom," Susan corrected him.

Thomas squinted at her. "What are you, Miss Piggy or something?"

"By a big, angry basketball player," Gary said.

Thomas looked back at the game. "Don't see any."

Susan yawned. Thomas skated backwards in a small circle in front of them, then did a pirouette, then skated on one foot with his other leg stretched out behind him. Susan and Gary pretended they weren't watching.

"You can act like you're not interested," Thomas said, "but I know something that you'd really like to know."

Susan continued to work on her cuticles and Gary made like he was intensely interested in the basketball game.

Thomas skated so close to the bench he almost ran over Gary's foot. "About a phone call from some guy who needs a band," he said, making a wide circle in front of them. "Except I think Mom told him she didn't know of any bands who'd be interested." Then Gary's brother skated away, picking up speed and zooming through the basketball game again. One of the players tried to throw the ball at him, but Thomas dodged it gracefully and disappeared out the entrance of the playground.

Susan looked up from her cuticles. "Why is he so obnoxious?" she asked.

But Gary was in shock. "Did you hear what he said? Someone called because they need a band!"

Susan didn't look surprised. "So? I told you something would come up." She went back to work on her nails.

•

Later that night Gary spoke to a Mr. McCann at someplace in Brooklyn called the Pin Club. The club was planning a Memorial Day weekend bash—four different bands every night for three nights, twelve bands in all. One of the scheduled bands had canceled and they needed a replacement. Mr. McCann said a friend had given him the Electric Outlet's tape and he'd liked it. Of course, Mr. McCann said, he wanted an experienced band with a track record at other clubs. Of course, Gary replied and promptly named six clubs, five of which the Electric Outlet had never played at. Fine, Mr. McCann said, have your manager call me and we'll discuss the arrangements. Before Gary could respond, Mr. McCann hung up.

For a moment Gary considered calling Mr. McCann back and explaining that the band didn't have a manager. But it wouldn't sound right, especially for a band that had allegedly played gigs at six other clubs. Gary wanted to talk it over with Susan, but she'd gone out again with

Michael and he had no idea when she'd get home. He called Karl's.

"Twelve bands for one weekend?" Karl said after Gary told him what was up. "Sounds like a big deal."

"Have you ever heard of this place—the Pin Club?" Gary asked.

Karl had to admit that he hadn't. "Maybe it's new or something."

"Well, anyway," Gary said, "this guy wants to talk to our manager. I didn't want to tell him we didn't have one."

There was a pause on the phone, then Karl said. "What do you want to do, put an ad in the paper or something?"

But Gary had an idea. "What about your mom?" he asked.

"I don't think she knows any managers," Karl said.

"No, Karl, what I mean is, maybe she'd like to be our manager."

"My mother?" Karl asked.

"Sure," Gary said. "She likes the band. I bet she'd be good."

"Aw, come off it, Gary," Karl said. "It's bad enough I have to live with her. Now you want her to manage my band too?"

"Listen," Gary said. "We'll just do it to impress the guy. She doesn't really have to be our manager. We'll just pretend so we can get this job. Come on, Karl, we need it."

Karl agreed reluctantly and got off the phone to ask his mother if she'd do it. A few moments later he was back on. "Okay, she said she'd love to do it." He didn't sound happy.

"Great," Gary said.

"And she says she won't even ask for a cut of the action," Karl added.

"Uh, okay."

"But she said she would like to meet with the band to discuss its long-term plans and goals."

"Uh, that's okay too," Gary said hesitantly.

Karl just groaned. "I'm telling you, Gary, you don't know what you're getting us into."

Thirteen

For starters, Mrs. Roesch got them into the Pin Club for $150 for one show. Not only was that more than the band had ever earned in a single night, but it meant that Gary could now call Cat's Eye Studios and tell them to go ahead and press their record.

It was a long subway ride to Brooklyn on Memorial Day, but the band was glad to make it. As the dirty, dimly lit subway train rattled and lurched along its underground tracks, Karl sat next to Gary, reading *The Village Voice.* Across the subway aisle from them sat Oscar and Susan, their instrument cases and Oscar's ironing board tucked safely under their legs. Oscar was talking to Susan and pointing to the top of his head, but Gary couldn't hear what he was saying in the steady roar. He watched as Oscar took a huge yellow tablet twice the size of an M & M from a pill bottle and swallowed it.

"Hey," Karl yelled at him. "Got any more?"

Oscar scowled. "They're vitamins, dimwit," he yelled back. "For my hair."

"What happened to the electric shock treatment?" Gary yelled.

Oscar shook his head and yelled back. "Didn't work. But this is guaranteed. It's a special formula that's supposed to stimulate hair growth. I take four a day." Then he tilted his head toward Gary. As far as Gary could tell, Oscar's hair looked thinner than ever. Oscar looked up again. "Think it's helping?"

"It's hard to tell," Gary shouted. Oscar looked disappointed.

"You ever consider a toupee?" Karl yelled.

Oscar frowned. "Did you ever consider sanding your face with an electric sander?" he shouted back.

Karl stopped smiling. "Listen, twerp," he yelled across the car. "These zits'll go away someday. But once you're bald, you're bald for good."

"Well, I'd rather be me bald than you, pimples or no pimples," Oscar yelled back.

Karl's face was turning red. "You know, you think you're superior to everyone," he shouted, "but you're not so great."

"Oh, yeah?" Oscar yelled. "Well, at least I can play piano. I've seen wind-up toys that played better drums than you."

Gary jumped up. "Stop it!" he shouted. "Enough. I don't know what's wrong with you guys. Here we are finally getting gigs again and all you can do is fight. Come on, we have to stick together now."

Karl and Oscar both shrugged. Then Karl got up and said he was going to go have a smoke. The three other members of the band watched him walk down to the end of the aisle and go out into the space between cars. Gary picked up the *Voice* and sat down next to Susan and Oscar.

"There he goes getting stoned again," Oscar grumbled. "And in the meantime he can't even come up with his share of the money for our single."

"Don't worry, Oscar," Gary said, looking through the paper. "After tonight we'll have it."

The lead article in the music section of the *Voice* was headlined ZOOMING TO THE TOP. It was a story about the Zoomies by Mike Wexler, the paper's legendary rock critic. Gary felt himself turning green with envy. Mike Wexler had single-handedly brought to the attention of the world at least half a dozen now-famous groups or musicians. A rave review by him practically insured a record contract with one of the big record companies like Columbia or Warner or Arista. But Mike Wexler's rave reviews were few and far between.

Gary quickly read the article and was surprised to find Wexler's review of the Zoomies only lukewarm. "Will there be no end to these skin-deep glittering show bands that now dominate rock and New Wave?" he wrote. However, another part of the article said, "I have no doubt that if the Zoomies continue to follow this now almost patented formula of flashy stage antics and excessively loud, simple music, they will succeed at all they aspire to."

Millionaires before the age of twenty, Gary thought. Then he turned to the nightclub listings in the back of the paper and saw that the Zoomies had no fewer than six different club dates in New York during June alone. And two of the dates were at big clubs where they were opening for well-known "name" acts. Suddenly, being one of twelve bands to play at the Pin Club in Brooklyn that weekend didn't seem so great.

"Look at this," he said, showing the paper to Susan.

Susan read through the listings and nudged Oscar. "Gary's going into his Zoomie fixation again."

"The Zoomies stink," Oscar yelled at Gary.

"You think they ever played at the Pin Club?" Gary asked.

"Probably worse," Susan replied.

But had Susan been able to see into the future she might not have been so sure.

•

"A bowling alley?" Karl asked, incredulous.

Gary thought there must have been a mistake until he saw the large sign outside the alley. There in *big* red plastic letters it said:

PIN CLUB MEMORIAL DAY WEEKEND BASH
FOUR NEW BANDS EVERY NIGHT!
Appearing Tonight

SON OF A GUN
SPERMAZOIDS
THE LIVING BRAS *(All Girl)*
THE ELECTRIC OUTLET

The band stood in the parking lot of the Pin Club, gaping at the sign in various states of disbelief. After a while, Oscar turned to the rest of the group. "I think it is ridiculous to play in a bowling alley," he said firmly.

Next to him, Karl nodded. "I hate to agree with anything Oscar says," he said, "but I never heard of playing in a bowling alley."

Gary couldn't really argue. All he could imagine was the band trying to play amid loud crashes of bowling pins as Pin Club regulars threw strikes down the alleys around them.

Only Susan was brave enough to carry on. "Come on," she said, picking up her bass and laughing. "Maybe we'll even get a few free games before the show."

Inside, the Pin Club was brightly lit. It looked like a normal bowling alley, except that where there should have been people bowling and the sounds of pins crashing, there were half a dozen kids scurrying around setting up chairs, while a short man with long tufts of gray hair growing from the sides of his head and a long unlit cigar jammed in his mouth screamed orders at them.

"Frank, you get those alleys swept yet?" he barked. "Where're you going with those cases of Coke, Barry? I told you, the refreshment stand. And you," he shouted at a third, "put those chairs out like I told you!"

The short man with the cigar turned around and saw Gary and the band. "Never again!" he screamed at them. "Look at this!" he gestured at a wooden bowling alley spotted with tiny brown dots. "They put out cigarettes in the bowling alley!" he yelled. "This alley is ruined. Those animals. They dropped bowling balls in the toilets. They broke windows. They poured beer down the ball retriever!"

Gary, Susan, Oscar, and Karl didn't know what to do except nod in sympathy as the little man continued to scream at them.

"My brother Sam," he yelled. "My brilliant brother Sam. I told him, 'Sam, the place'll get wrecked, you have these kids in here for three nights.' Sam, wonderful Sam, says, 'No, Louie, they're good kids. They won't break anything!' Then he says, 'Think of the money, Louie! In three nights you'll make more than three months of bowling!' So now I'm thinking of the money all right. I'm thinking of the money it's gonna cost to fix forty-six bowling alleys, the money to fix the toilets, the money to fix the ball retriever. Yeah, I'm thinking of the money all right. Let me tell you, the next time I see that brother of mine I'm gonna . . ." The little man made an obscene gesture with his arm.

Meanwhile, Gary and the band stood stunned. Having finished his tirade, the man squinted at them. "What do you kids want?" he demanded.

"We're the Electric Outlet," Gary said.

"Oh, yeah? Well, congratulations." The man smirked. Then he pointed to the other side of the building. "The dressing room is down there past the shoe rental. Be ready for a sound check in an hour. Meantimes, don't wander around—I already got enough to worry about."

The dressing room was jammed with people. The mixture of marijuana and cigarette smoke was so thick Oscar started coughing. There were so many people in there that Gary couldn't believe they were all in bands. The weird thing was, you couldn't tell who was and who wasn't. Everyone looked like a musician. All around the room people were strumming guitars, girls were singing song phrases, guys with drumsticks were tapping out rhythms on the metal lockers. Altogether they made an incredible racket.

Clutching their instrument cases tightly, Gary and the band picked their way through the crowd to a corner in the back of the locker room. There they sat in a tight little circle and gaped at the musical mob.

"Can you believe it?" Susan asked.

"What a zoo," Oscar said.

"It's like a festival," Karl said. "I'll bet it's like this backstage at Madison Square Garden."

To their right, someone laughed and said in a deep, hoarse voice, "Don't bet on it." Gary turned and saw a woman wearing skintight black pants and a tight pink top sitting on the floor near them. Her eyes were almost black with makeup, her lips were bright red, and her hair was bleached blond. She held a long, thin cigarette in her left hand.

"Why not?" Susan asked her.

"Because, honey," she said, "most of this menagerie has never performed in its life."

"Then what are they doing here?" Gary asked.

The lady shrugged. "They're roadies, groupies, hangers-on, friends, cousins, distant relatives, mothers, fathers—you name it. They come and hang out in the dressing room and pretend they're musicians."

Oscar, Susan, Gary, and Karl looked around the room once more, but it was impossible to tell where the bands ended and the groupies began. The lady smiled. Gary noticed she had small yellow teeth. "By the way"—she held out her hand toward Gary—"I'm Patty LaThong, lead singer with the Living Bras. You must be the Electric Outlet."

"How'd you guess?" Gary asked as he shook Patty's hand.

Patty pointed at a group of strangely dressed people with her long cigarette. They were all wearing brightly colored shirts and vests and strange caps on their heads. "That's the Spermazoid party," she said. Then she pointed to a tough-looking group wearing torn denim or leather jackets and black jeans and leather boots. "They're associated with Son of a Gun." Then she pointed to a group nearer to them. These were mostly women in garish outfits like Patty's. "This is the Living Bra contingent. Some show, huh?"

The Electric Outlet nodded.

Patty LaThong turned out to be a pretty good show, too, as she told the band the story of her musical career. She said she couldn't even remember how many bands she'd been in. She'd been in hippie bands, soul bands, heavy metal, rhythm and blues, country Western, acid rock, punk, New Wave, old wave. "Right now," she said, touching her long, bleached-blond hair, "I guess I'm into permanent wave."

Gary didn't ask how long she'd been performing, but when Patty said that her first band had once opened for the Young Rascals he got a pretty good idea. Patty had to be at least twice his age.

The all-girl Living Bras had been together for about four years, and when Gary asked if they were successful, Patty said, "About as successful as the other bands here. We cut an album a couple of years ago. It did okay, but the record company didn't ask us to do another." There was a tinge of melancholy in her voice.

"Do you still enjoy it?" Susan asked.

"Oh, I don't know." Patty sighed. "I've been doing it for so long now . . ."

"Do you ever think about doing something else?" asked Karl.

Patty smiled. "All the time, honey. But what else is there? I'm too old to start having kids. The only thing I know how to do is sing. Besides, even after all this time I still tell myself that tomorrow might be our big break."

"I hope so," Susan said.

Patty LaThong didn't say anything. She just smiled at Susan. Somehow Gary got the feeling that she already knew she was going to spend the rest of her days singing in places like the Pin Club.

A little while later a gravelly voice yelled, "Shaddup!" and the locker room grew quiet. Down at the other end of the room Gary could see Mr. McCann. "All right," the little man shouted. "We're starting sound checks. You come out in the order you perform. That's the Electronic Outlet first. Either you're out in time for the sound check or you miss it. Got that? No more than ten minutes per sound check, so ya better set up fast or ya ain't gonna play. Okay? Any questions?"

"Yeah," said one member of the Spermazoid contingent. "How about a buffet, huh? We're hungry."

"Yeah, where's the beer?" yelled a Son of a Gun.

McCann glared at them. "You want food, go across the street and get some. This ain't no goddamn party."

"Hey," someone yelled. "I've played in holes worse than this dump and at least they gave us beer."

"Yeah? Well, go back to your holes," Mr. McCann snarled and left. No sooner was he out of the room than someone picked up an old bowling pin and threw it through one of the windows above the lockers. There was a loud crash, and several people had to jump out of the way of flying glass. Mr. McCann was back in the room in an instant. "Who did that?" he screamed.

No one said a word. The Electric Outlet stared at each other in disbelief.

"All right," Mr. McCann yelled. "One more incident and I'll have the cops in here. We'll cancel the show and throw you all in jail." He left again. There were a few grumbles, but the crowd suddenly became peaceful.

"What's going on?" Oscar asked Patty.

The singer coughed. "Just about everyone in here is carrying enough dope to get five to ten in the slammer, honey."

"Come on," Susan said, taking the Fender bass out of its case. "We better get ready to do the sound check." Gary got out his Stratocaster and Karl helped Oscar with his keyboard. They started to leave the locker room, but Patty stopped them.

"You better take those cases with you," she said, pointing at the guitar cases the band was leaving behind.

"But we'll be back in ten minutes," Gary said.

"I promise you they won't be there if you leave them," Patty said.

The band picked up the cases and Patty gave them a few more tips. "Make sure you get paid in cash tonight, kids," she said. "Don't take a check from anyone. And have them call a cab for you. Don't even wait outside for it. Wait inside until it comes and then take it all the way to the city."

"How come?" Karl asked.

"You walk out on the street after dark with your equipment and your pockets full of cash and I guarantee you you'll be unwilling participants in a free giveaway," Patty said.

"Oh, God," Oscar moaned.

Patty smiled. "Welcome to the wonderful world of entertainment, kids."

•

The show that night was one of the most terrifying experiences in the band's career. An enormous, raucous crowd jammed the bowling alley, and as the band performed Gary watched in amazement as kids who couldn't have been more than eleven or twelve swallowed handfuls of brightly colored pills and washed them down with beer or wine. Fights broke out all around them and a guy who'd drunk too much threw up. Kids were shouting at the band and some of them tried to climb up on the stage, but they were thrown off by McCann's bouncers.

About halfway through their act, a bowling ball flashed across the stage, knocking Oscar off his feet before it smashed into the shoe rental desk. The music stopped as Gary and Susan rushed to help Oscar up. "You okay?"

"I think so." Oscar was unhurt, but he was white as a sheet and trembling as they helped him to his feet. Meanwhile, Mr. McCann had climbed up on the stage and was shouting into the band's microphone. *"Anyone caught trying to knock over members of the bands with bowling balls will be thrown out of the concert."*

"Somehow, I don't feel reassured," Gary mumbled as he returned to his microphone. The band started playing again and soon more objects— empty bottles, beer cans, and someone's sneaker —were sailing toward the stage. Suddenly a half-full can of beer bounced off the wall behind Karl, soaking him. The crowd hooted and laughed as the Electric Outlet's drummer jumped up and wiped the beer from his hair and face. There was fury in Karl's eyes as he picked up the bowling ball that had knocked Oscar down and stood at the edge of the stage, swinging the ball wildly in the air as if at any second he would fling it straight into the disruptive crowd. The effect was impressive. The crowd shut up, and the band finished its set and left the stage without another incident.

Fourteen

Alaska, Arizona, Arkansas, Delaware, Idaho, Illinois, Indiana, Iowa, Kansas, Kentucky, Louisiana, Michigan, Minnesota, Mississippi, Missouri, Montana, Nebraska, Nevada, New Hampshire, North Carolina, North Dakota, Ohio, Oklahoma, Oregon, Pennsylvania, South Dakota, Utah, Washington, West Virginia, Wisconsin, and Wyoming.

Gary closed the small green book on the laws of engagement and marriage. Well, it was pretty obvious. Thirty-one out of fifty states had laws against marrying your first cousin. And even though New York wasn't on the list, Gary didn't feel encouraged. When so many states were against it, you knew it couldn't be such a good thing. It all had to do with genetics. As the book explained, the offspring from the marriage of two first cousins might inherit the worst traits of both parents. Gary recalled seeing a show on television about an African tribe that had a lot of inter-marriage and wound up with a bunch of people with six fingers or toes. Of course, the riffs a six-fingered guitarist might be able to play could be incredible. But you couldn't count on that.

Gary looked forlornly around the Lenox Prep library, a musty room filled with old wooden fur-niture and green glass lamps and lined with walls of dusty bookcases. It didn't matter that much. He really wasn't *that* serious about Susan. It was just that, well, there weren't even *any other possibili-ties.* When he tried to think about a girl he could like, he either drew a blank or thought of his cousin. But to be truthful, even before he'd come to the library he'd known it was hopeless with Susan. More than half the states in the country were against it and Susan didn't exactly seem interested either. The only person Gary thought might like the idea was his mother. If Gary and Susan got together, she wouldn't have to worry all the time about whom Susan was going out with.

Gary noticed that Mrs. Edelman, the Lenox Prep librarian, was headed toward his table with an armload of books. When he'd first gone into the library that afternoon, Gary had asked her where he could find information on relationships between first cousins and Mrs. Edelman had sent him to the law section for the book on laws of engagement and marriage. Now the tall, bespectacled woman piled six books in front of him and picked up the top one.

"There's an article in here about children born to first cousins," she said. "I've marked the page." Then she picked up the next book and the next, going through the pile and explaining why she'd chosen each one. "This is about Queen Victoria and Prince Albert. I believe they were first cousins. This one is about Franklin and Eleanor Roosevelt and this one is about an old German royal family, the Hapsburgs, who often married cousins. This last one is about Toulouse-Lautrec."

"Wasn't he an artist or something?" Gary asked.

"Yes," said Mrs. Edelman. "I believe his parents were first cousins. Mr. Toulouse-Lautrec was slightly crippled and his parents blamed themselves for it."

"Oh," Gary said, not exactly welcoming the news. "Well, uh, thanks a lot for finding all these books for me."

"You're welcome, Gary," Mrs. Edelman said. She paused at the table. "May I ask if this is for a school project?"

"Uh, no, it's personal research," Gary said.

Mrs. Edelman gave him a funny look. "Well," she said. "I hope you'll find what you're looking for. If you need any more help, just ask."

Gary thanked her and she walked away. The only book he bothered reading was the one with the article about children born to first cousins. It said they were about twelve times more likely to have serious illnesses than normal children. That was all he had to know. The last thing in the world he needed was a bunch of sniffling, coughing kids who contracted the mumps, measles, and chicken pox the way normal kids scraped their knees. Just the idea that if he and Susan got married they could never have kids who were considered "normal" was bad enough. And it certainly wasn't fair to increase the risk of having a crippled kid either—even if he could be a great painter.

Closing the book, Gary thought about the guys in his class. A lot of them had steady girl friends. Or if they didn't have one steady girl, at least they went out a lot. That is, if they weren't total nerds. Gary was pretty sure that not many of them were virgins either.

Somehow he'd fallen behind. And it wasn't just a matter of getting laid either. The point was, other guys in his class were going out with girls and having a good time. When it came to doing social stuff, they were *progressing*. But Gary wasn't. If anything, he was *regressing*.

And no one else in his band was any different. In one way or another, they were all in the same boat. Oscar was weird. He didn't even talk about girls. He acted as if they didn't exist. Karl knew they existed, but he was so hung up about his zits that he was certain no one would ever go out with him. Susan's problem went to the exact opposite extreme. To Gary she seemed too involved. Especially with this Michael guy. It seemed that these days she lived only to see him. Everything else was unimportant.

And Gary—what exactly was his problem? Well, it wasn't really a problem, he told himself. He just didn't have much time. He had to practice guitar alone every day and rehearse with the band. And then there were the millions of little administrative chores he had to do, like trying to line up gigs and talking to Cat's Eye Studios about their record and making sure everyone showed up for rehearsals.

But still, he'd had opportunities. And not just with Kathy, who'd taken him home that night, or the girl in the white vest at the SoHo party. Other girls had stayed after gigs to talk with him. Some of them had seemed pretty nice, but somehow he'd always been too busy and preoccupied with the band. It was more important to be a rock star first. The girls would come later.

But a thought lingered in his mind. He couldn't help wondering why so many other guys had girl friends, while he hadn't gone out with anyone in almost two years. Could it be that he was a little scared? Gary shook his head. Aw, the hell with it, he thought. He was playing amateur psychiatrist again, only instead of trying to figure out someone else, he was trying to figure himself out. That was dumb. If musicians were normal people, then they probably wouldn't be musicians. You had to be a little crazy. That was what "Rock Therapy" was all about.

A tall, thin guy with long red hair, wearing a black "Clash" T-shirt, walked past the library door carrying a bright orange sack over his shoulder. It took Gary a second to realize it was Karl. He got up and went out in the hall.

"Hey, Karl!"

Karl turned and waved when he saw Gary.

"What are you doing here?" Gary asked.

"I was in the neighborhood, so I thought I'd visit the old alma mater," Karl said. "I was looking for you."

Gary glanced around. Except for them, the hallway was empty. It was class time and you weren't supposed to be in the halls. "Come on," Gary said. "Let's go in the library." They went back to the table where Gary'd been sitting.

"So, what's happening?" Gary asked.

Karl shrugged. "Nothing much. I had to make a delivery to some guy's apartment at Park and Seventy-eighth Street, so I thought I'd stop by. What's happening with the record?"

"It should be ready late next week or the week after," Gary said.

Karl shook his head. "Unreal," he said. "Our own single. Maybe if we get enough steady gigs after that I'll be able to quit this dumb job." He gestured at the orange messenger's sack.

"Stinks, huh?"

"The pits," Karl said. He was gazing at the pile

of books on the table. Gary realized he'd left them open. "Hey, what's this?" Karl asked, staring at the book in front of him. "Children of first cousins more prone to disease?" He looked up at Gary and gasped, "With Susan? You didn't, did you?"

"You're right, I didn't," Gary said.

Karl scowled. "But then, why read . . ." He gasped again. "You're planning to?"

Gary sighed. "Gimme a break, Karl."

"Well, then I don't get it," Karl said.

Gary shrugged. It was probably better to tell Karl the truth than to leave it up to his imagination. "I was just wondering, that's all."

"Oh, yeah, I see," Karl said. But he had a funny smile on his face. "I guess we all wonder once in a while, huh?"

"Yeah." Gary felt mortified.

At least Karl was sensitive enough not to push the topic any further. Instead, he looked around the library. "Three weeks and it's all over, huh?"

Gary nodded.

Karl looked down at the orange messenger's bag again. "Maybe I should have stayed in school this year. All the guys I work with are just like me—high school dropouts. There's this one guy, Angelo. I swear he must be thirty-five years old. Thirty-five and all he does all day is deliver packages. I mean . . . talk about dead ends."

Gary was suddenly aware of another person nearby and looked up to see Mrs. Edelman standing behind them. She was looking at Karl. "Mr.

Roesch," the librarian said, "I believe that you are no longer a student here."

"I'm just visiting, Mrs. Edelman," Karl said.

"I'm afraid that visits by outsiders are not allowed," Mrs. Edelman said sternly. "You'll have to go now."

"I'm not an outsider," Karl said. "I went here for three years."

"But you don't go here anymore, Mr. Roesch," the librarian said. "And considering that during the three years you were here you never set foot in this library, I can't imagine what business you could have here today."

"Maybe I'm thinking about coming back so I can use it," Karl said.

Mrs. Edelman smiled. "Well, then, you ought to go down to the headmaster's office and talk it over with him."

Gary got up. "Come on, Karl, I'll walk you out. I gotta go to class soon anyway."

Karl got up slowly, and as he and Gary passed Mrs. Edelman she said, "Maybe we'll see you next year."

"Yeah, maybe," Karl said.

Fifteen

In the middle of a busy downtown record store, the bearded, burly store manager handed the Electric Outlet's first single back to Gary. "What can I tell ya?" he said. "We don't take independently produced singles." Gary stared down at the record in his hands. The jacket was nothing more than a white sheath of paper with a poorly drawn picture of an electric wall socket with some musical notes floating out of it. It had to be the dumbest-looking record jacket Gary had ever seen, and he was certain every record store manager who saw it thought so too.

Gary looked back at the man in a sort of daze. Actually, he was exhausted. It was Saturday evening and he'd been on his feet since 10:00 that morning, carrying a shoe box full of singles from record store to record store, trying to sell them. But he had not sold a record all day. He had not even been able to give one away.

"Uh, listen," the manager said. His long black hair was pulled back into a ponytail, and something about him made Gary think that he too was an aspiring musician when he wasn't managing the store. "This store is part of an enormous chain all over the country. We don't buy records ourselves. The regional office buys 'em. We just get shipments of records. We don't even know what we're getting from one week to the next. Except all the records come from the big companies. And they're all on the charts."

Gary nodded. He had heard the same story all day—all week, in fact. Managers in store after store had told him, "You gotta have radio play, you have to be on the charts. We don't buy the records ourselves. You gotta be signed with the big record companies." Gary couldn't even remember all the stores he'd been to or how many blocks he'd walked. His memory was mush.

"Listen," the store manager said. "Don't think I don't know what you're going through. I'm in a band myself and we got three singles. You think I can put my own singles in this store? Forget it. The regional manager comes in here and sees my record in the racks and I'm out lookin' for a new job. You gotta understand—we get kids like you comin' off the street with homemade singles every day of the week." The manager paused and looked around the store. Here comes the brush-off, Gary thought. The manager looked back at him. "I'll tell you what, though," he said. "There's a store in the Village, Bleecker Joe's. Sometimes he takes a record if he likes it. Why don't you try him?"

Why? Gary thought. Because I've already tried him. Bleecker Joe's was his first stop four days ago when he started carrying the shoe box of records around. Bleecker Joe had listened to the record right there in the store and bought ten copies. But that had been Gary's first and last sale of the week. He could only hope that one of the other members of the band had had better luck.

Meanwhile, the manager was starting to look nervous. "Uh, look, kid, I got a store to manage. I'm real sorry, you know?" Gary thanked him and turned away from the counter where the manager stood. At least the guy was nice about it, he thought wearily as he trudged out of the store. The box of records felt heavy under his arm. He'd been carrying it for four days. It was almost seven o'clock and he headed toward home, sorely tempted to throw the box of records into the next trash can he saw.

•

That night before dinner, Susan, Gary, and Thomas were sitting around the table. Dr. Specter was on the phone and Mrs. Specter was in the kitchen. "Any luck?" Susan whispered. She knew Gary didn't want his parents to find out about the record. They'd have a fit if they found out he'd used all his savings to pay for his share of it.

Gary shook his head. "What about you?"

Susan said she'd done no better. "I tried, Gary," she said. "But I felt so dumb going into those stores with this little record in my hand. I kept asking myself, Why would they want this? They don't even know who the Electric Outlet is."

Gary nodded sadly. At least Susan was honest about it.

"What are you talking about?" Thomas asked.

Gary glanced at his brother. "We made a record of some of our songs," he said quietly.

"You got a record!" Thomas shouted. At that moment Mrs. Specter walked in carrying a roast chicken.

"What are you yelling about, Thomas?" she asked.

"Uh, I bought a new record today," Gary said, and at the same time he made a fist at Thomas to indicate that he would suffer brute force if he uttered another word.

"I wish you wouldn't spend all your money on records, Gary," his mother said halfheartedly and went back into the kitchen.

"Can I have a copy?" Thomas whispered.

"Okay," Gary hissed. "Just keep your mouth shut."

·

Later Gary was walking through the kitchen when he heard Thomas on the phone. "Yeah," his brother was saying in a hushed voice. "It's a real record. You wanna hear it?" Gary watched as his little brother grabbed his jacket and, record in hand, dashed out the door.

That evening Gary sought refuge in the Shrine of the Rock-and-Roll Guitarist. He plugged his headphones into his stereo and put on an old Byrds album. Then he sat on the floor next to his bed and engaged in depression activity—looking at pictures of rock-and-roll stars on the covers of their albums.

What a difference there was between the covers of the albums and the cover of the Electric Outlet's first single. Gary got mad when he thought about their record. The cover looked exactly like the kind of thing a bunch of high school kids would put out. It had never occurred to him to check the art Cat's Eye Studios would put on their single. There were so many things in this business that you'd never think of doing.

A little later Gary noticed that the door to his room was opening slowly. He saw blond hair, and then Susan stuck her head in. Her lips were moving, but with the headphones on his ears, all Gary could hear was Roger McGuinn singing, "*So you want to be a rock-and-roll star . . .*" Susan was wearing a blue silk blouse and tight jeans and her face was all made up. Her lips were still moving. Gary wondered what she was saying.

Susan reached over and turned off the stereo.

Silence.

Gary sat motionless with the headphones still

over his ears. He didn't really want to hear what Susan was going to say. He didn't want to see, feel, or hear anything. He wished he was in an intergalactic space shuttle one hundred billion light-years away.

"Gary." Susan had to shout. "Please take those things off your head. I want to talk to you."

Gary slowly took the earphones off. "I know what you're going to say," he told her. "You're going to tell me that the record stores won't take our record because it isn't getting any airplay from the radio stations. They do it on purpose, Susan. They set it up so we can't win. The radio station won't play the record unless it's in the stores and the stores won't sell the record unless the radio station plays it. It's a plot. The sole purpose of ninety-nine percent of the bands in this world is to provide money for rehearsal and recording studios, to keep rock magazines in business, and to be targets for flying sneakers and bowling balls. It's a vicious cycle preying on naïve young bands who are dumb enough to think they can make it."

Susan bent her head slightly and was quiet for a moment. She seemed to smile quizzically.

"That's not what I came in here to talk about," she said. "I came in here to talk about a certain rock guitarist I know who still fantasizes about marrying his first cousin."

Gary blinked and a thought slowly formed in his brain: he would kill Karl Roesch.

"And please don't blame Karl, either," Susan said, as if she could read his mind. "It just slipped out by accident."

"I bet," Gary said sourly.

Susan sat down on his bed. "Gary, I thought all of that ended years ago. What happened that night is over. It was a mistake and I thought we learned our lesson."

Gary was so embarrassed he couldn't talk. He just sat there feeling his cheeks turn red. For a while he and Susan looked at each other without speaking. Hearing it from Susan's lips, Gary had to admit it did sound silly.

"Uh, let me explain," Gary stammered. "I wasn't really that serious about it. I was just, like, well, er, you know, curious. I had a school period with nothing to do so I went down to the library and looked at a couple of books. I mean, I know what happened was an accident. I guess I was just feeling that way because you're the only girl I—aw—I don't know." Gary's face burned.

Susan smiled and knelt beside her cousin. "You're such a nut, Gary. What about those girls who used to hang around you at the Rock Garden? What was wrong with them?"

Gary shrugged and pushed some hair out of his eyes. "Aw, I don't know."

"You know what I think," Susan said. "I think you're afraid. So you picked an impossible person like your cousin so you wouldn't have to face any real possibilities."

"Thank you, Miss Amateur Psychiatrist," Gary said glumly.

Susan laughed. "You're welcome, Mr. Crazy Cousin. The only thing I can't understand about you, Gary, is why you don't have a million girl friends."

"It must be the mouthwash I'm using," Gary mumbled.

"There, you see," said Susan. "You refuse to even talk about other girls seriously. And I know at least two girls who'd—"

"No, don't say it," Gary interrupted her. "You know two girls who'd both love to meet me and they're both beautiful and neither one plays the tuba."

"The tuba?" Susan frowned.

Gary stood up. "Look, I'm sorry about what happened. I know it was a dumb thing to do. I just, I don't know." He didn't really know what to say and he was still horribly embarrassed, so he held out his hand. "Friends?"

Susan got up and kissed him on the cheek. "It's Saturday night. Aren't you going out?" she asked.

Gary shook his head. "I got four finals and a paper due next week, and I haven't even begun to study," he said.

"Suit yourself." Susan headed for the door. But then she stopped as if she had another thought. "And by the way, Gary. You know what you said about young bands just providing money for studios?"

"Yeah?"

"Well, it may be true for everyone else, but it's not true for you." She pulled the door closed and was gone.

Sixteen

For one week Gary forgot about music and concentrated on school. Somewhat. For his final project in poetry writing he handed in the lyrics of all the songs he'd written that year, and his term paper for music history compared the musical development of Mozart with that of John Lennon. Geometry, U.S. history, and physics were all straight grinds, but he found that if he crammed for an hour, then listened to an album for twenty minutes, he could study for most of the evening without going berserk.

When it was all over, one day in the middle of June, Gary walked out of Lenox Prep for the last time. He might have to return for commencement exercises and graduation, but as far as he was concerned, high school was over. He had no date for the senior prom.

For several days following, Gary's life consisted

of practicing guitar, rehearsing with the band, and playing a couple of hours of basketball every afternoon. Around the Specter household the end of the school year traditionally marked the beginning of a summer job, but this summer Gary showed no signs of looking for work. Polite inquiries from his mother as to when he was going to start looking for a summer job were met with equally polite responses that he would start looking just as soon as Operation WHAT was over.

"What?" Gary's mother asked.

"That's right," Gary said. "Operation WHAT. W-H-A-T."

Apparently this answer did not satisfy Mrs. Specter, and one afternoon she brought out the heavy artillery to get the truth.

Thomas ran ahead to the playground to warn Gary, who was practicing lay-ups at the basket while waiting for some guys to arrive for a game. Gary saw his little brother and couldn't believe it. For the first time in months Thomas wasn't on roller skates.

"Mom and Dad are coming," Thomas said, catching his breath. Gary took a jump shot, rebounded the ball, and went in for a lay-up. He didn't have to ask his brother why they were coming. Meanwhile, Thomas reached into his pocket and pulled something out. He stepped onto the court and handed a bunch of crumpled bills to his brother.

"How much?" Gary asked.

"Six," said Thomas. It was part of a new deal Thomas had suggested. He was selling copies of the Electric Outlet's single to his friends for $1.50 and then giving Gary a dollar while keeping fifty cents as commission. As far as Gary could tell, it didn't matter to his brother's friends what songs were on the record—it was just the idea that Thomas's brother had a record that made it sell.

Across the playground, Gary's mother and father appeared. Dr. Specter was dressed in his light blue dental smock. Mrs. Specter must have dragged him out of his office. His parents stopped at the side of the court as Gary banked one in off the backboard.

"Gary," his mother said. "I assume that you are making no effort toward finding a summer job."

Gary stopped dribbling and wiped some sweat off his forehead with the front of his T-shirt. "That's true," he said.

"We feel that as your parents," his mother said, "we have a right to know what you plan to do this summer."

"I told you, Mom—I'll look for a job just as soon as I've completed my current project," Gary said. He double-pumped and tried to lay one up with his left hand. The ball missed the basket completely.

"And how long will it take to complete your current project?" his mother asked.

"I don't know, Mom—it's not all up to me," Gary said. He sank a hook shot.

"Good shot," said Dr. Specter. Gary's mother frowned at her husband.

"You know most of the jobs get taken early in the summer," his mother said. "By the time you're ready to look, there may not be any jobs available."

"I'll take my chances," Gary said. He tried the left-handed double pump and missed again.

Mrs. Specter turned to her husband. "Don't you have anything to say?" she asked desperately.

Dr. Specter thought for a moment. "I think he ought to try a simple left-handed lay-up first and, once he's mastered that, try double-pumping."

Gary's mother glared at her husband and Dr. Specter realized that wasn't exactly what she had wanted him to say. "I, uh, also think you should get a summer job," he told Gary.

Gary stopped dribbling again and walked over to his parents. "I will, Dad, just as soon as Operation WHAT is finished."

"What?" said Dr. Specter.

"That's right," Gary said. "WHAT. W-H-A-T."

"Would you mind telling us what Operation WHAT is?" his mother asked.

"Top Secret," Gary said. "But I promise it won't be much longer. One way or the other, we'll know pretty soon." He dribbled to his left, then quickly spun around and hit a jumper from fifteen feet.

"I didn't know you were this good," Gary's father said.

Gary grinned. "I'm just lucky today. You want to try a shot?"

His father nodded and Gary passed the ball to him. Slowly and deliberately, Dr. Specter shot the ball from twenty feet out and it sank through the hoop with a swish.

"Wow, Dad," Thomas said. "I didn't know you could play."

Dr. Specter smiled sheepishly. "Oh, I played a little in college. Had a pretty good outside shot." Gary passed the ball to his father again, and Dr. Specter moved gracefully to his right, his blue dental smock ruffling and his leather street shoes scraping on the asphalt. He shot again and again the ball sailed cleanly through the hoop.

Now Thomas ran out onto the court, shouting, "Let me try!" He got the ball and shot, but it fell short of the hoop. Gary caught it and passed it to his father, who proceeded to sink his third shot in a row.

Meanwhile, Mrs. Specter stood on the sideline watching in disbelief. "Harold," she snapped at her husband, "we did not come out here to shoot baskets."

"Aw, Mom," Gary said. "Just let him take a few more shots."

"Yeah," said Thomas. "We're having fun."

Mrs. Specter shook her head hopelessly and turned and walked back toward the brownstone. Dr. Specter stayed and shot baskets with his two sons for several minutes more, until the assistant from his office ran out to remind him that he'd left a patient sitting in the dentist's chair with a half-filled cavity.

•

That evening the phone call Gary'd been waiting for came through.

"She did it," Karl said excitedly.

"Great," Gary said. "When can we see him?"

"Tonight before his show. The building's down on Third Avenue. You know the one. I'll meet you outside at ten."

WHAT was located in a skyscraper that took almost an entire city block. That night at ten, a guard let Karl and Gary into the building and then another guard escorted them to the floor where the radio station was located. The doors to WHAT were locked and the guard waited with them until Evan Walker appeared to let them in.

"Oh, yes, I remember you two," the disc jockey said as he led them down a hallway decorated with huge posters of popular rock groups like Styx, the Beatles, Heart, and Cheap Trick. They went through a door marked STUDIOS and past a row of glass-enclosed booths jammed with large green turntables and lots of electronic equipment.

Above one booth was a brightly lit red box proclaiming ON THE AIR, and as Walker passed he waved to a guy inside who was talking into a microphone while he changed records on one of two turntables beside him. The guy waved back to Walker with his free hand and continued talking. Outside in the hallway, Gary recognized the voice. He was Dickie Henderson, the DJ who preceded Evan Walker every night. Gary stopped and stared into the booth. Henderson had long curly brown hair that fell past his shoulders, and his wrists were adorned with silver and turquoise Indian jewelry. But what was really fascinating was that the voice Gary heard coming from the booth was also being broadcast over the radio to hundreds of thousands of listeners. And he was standing only a few feet from its source!

"Come on, Gary," Karl hissed, pulling him away. A couple of doors down, Evan Walker pushed one open and held it for them. Gary and Karl stepped into a small office crammed to the ceiling with reel-to-reel tape recorders, a stereo turntable and amp, speakers, and tape players. There were photographs of Walker with rock groups like the Eagles and Bob Seger. There were plaques and award certificates enclosed in glass frames and a row of golf trophies from the WHAT annual summer outing. There was also a large, childishly drawn crayon picture of a man in a dark suit with a goatee that vaguely resembled Evan Walker. Near the picture a child had written "This is my daddy," with an arrow pointing to the man. Evan Walker sat down behind a small desk, and Karl and Gary sat down in chairs opposite him.

Karl kept looking at the picture the child had

drawn. "Uh, my mom wants you to know she really appreciates your taking the time—" he mumbled.

Evan Walker nodded and glanced at the drawing too. Then he said, "So you've got a band."

"Youngest professional band in New York," Gary bragged.

"Been gigging anywhere?" Walker asked.

Gary and Karl looked at each other. "Uh, we played the Pin Club a few weeks ago and before that we were the house band at the Rock Garden," Gary said, although he was pretty sure Walker had never heard of either place.

"But we left because of artistic differences," Karl added.

"Artistic differences?" Walker raised an eyebrow. "Like what?"

"Well, we play a lot of original material and the manager wanted us to play Top 40 stuff," Gary explained.

"Any gigs coming up?" the disc jockey asked.

There was that audition in July at the new place downtown called Galaxy One. "Just a place downtown you probably never heard of," Gary said with a shrug.

Evan Walker cleared his throat. "And you've made a single of your two best songs," he said.

Gary pulled the single out of his pocket and handed it to Walker, saying, "I know the cover art is pretty bad, but the music inside is better."

Walker held the record in his hand and looked

at the cover. "I've seen better and worse," he said. He pulled the record out of the sleeve.

"Our sound engineer was Walter Sloves at Cat's Eye Studios," Gary said, hoping this might help impress Walker a little.

Evan Walker looked up at Gary, his lips pressed together. "Never heard of him," he said.

Gary and Karl watched as the disc jockey put the record on the turntable, then flicked some knobs and switches and placed the tone arm on the record's edge. A second later the beginning of "Rock Therapy" enveloped the room: *"You know, they say I'm lazy . . ."*

Evan Walker sat sideways from Gary and Karl. He was motionless, not even tapping a finger to the beat. Gary was sure Walker didn't like it. The song sounded so old. Gary had played it and listened to it so many times that it almost bored him now. Walker remained motionless through the first verse, then the second. After the guitar break he glanced at Gary for a moment and then looked away. The song ended. Evan Walker scratched the skin beneath his goatee. "Who wrote it?" he asked.

"Me," Gary said.

"Music too?"

"No, Oscar writes the music," Gary said. "He's the piano player."

"And he's only sixteen," Karl added.

Walker nodded. "Your mother said you play drums, is that right?" he said to Karl, who said it was. Then the DJ turned to Gary. "And you, I take it, are the guitarist?"

"Yeah."

Walker nodded again, and Gary got the feeling he had seen a million bands just like them. The disc jockey flipped the record over and played "Educated Fool." Halfway through this song he pushed a button that made the record arm lift. Gary squirmed. Walker wasn't even going to listen to the whole side. The disc jockey turned to Gary. "The girl's a background singer?"

"She plays bass."

"She have any songs where she sings alone?"

"No, but she could."

Walker let the arm down again and finished listening to the song. When it was over, the disc jockey sat without moving except to stroke his goatee once in a while with his hand. He wasn't looking at either Gary or Karl, but out of the booth and into the hall. Gary was certain he was trying to figure out how to tell them nicely that the record wasn't very good, but Walker just sat there, as if lost in some thought cloud. Gary felt like he'd go nuts if the DJ didn't say something soon. Finally, Walker swiveled around in his chair and faced them. "How old are you, Gary?"

"Seventeen."

"You too?" he said to Karl.

"Uh-huh."

Evan Walker leaned back in his chair and looked at the small black record lying on the wide green felt turntable beside him. He touched the edge of the turntable and spun it around with his finger. "Picture yourself on a roulette wheel with ten thousand other bands," he said, staring at the plastic disc revolving in the middle of the turntable. "All spinning around, all trying to make it in rock and roll. How many will actually make it? You probably think the answer has to do with how good their music is." The disc jockey looked up and Gary and Karl nodded. "Well," Walker said "I'm afraid that's only a very small part of it. Even if all ten thousand bands were great, there just wouldn't be room for them. It would be economically unfeasible. Bands are too expensive. Musicians have to be paid, records have to be made and advertised, concerts have to be arranged, transportation, hotels, insurance. A record company can afford to support just a finite number of bands. Do you know how a record company decides which bands to produce?"

Gary and Karl shook their heads.

"Money," said Evan Walker. "The band's ability to make money is the most important, overriding factor. They can be great musicians or terrible musicians. But what it really comes down to is, can the band make money? Can they attract fans? That's it—the single most important fact in the music business."

Walker paused and Gary and Karl watched him uncomfortably.

"Now, what happens," the DJ went on, "is that

out of those ten thousand bands, perhaps two hundred are picked, each one on its potential to make money for the record company. For the other nine thousand, eight hundred bands it'll be bar gigs and small clubs and part-time jobs until they go on to something else.

"And even of the chosen two hundred, half will be flops—one-shot flashes in the pan, here this month, gone the next. Has-beens by the time they're thirty years old. Some will try to ride on fading glory, some will die of drug overdoses, the smart ones will take their money and run. A couple will even teach music."

"Or become disc jockeys," Karl said.

Walker smiled, but only for a moment. "Nothing in the world takes you as high as rock-and-roll stardom, but sooner or later you've got to fall. And the higher you've been, the harder you'll fall."

"Everyone says we're crazy to try it," Gary said.

Evan Walker shook his head. "No, you're not crazy. But just understand that the odds will always be against you. First, they'll be against you making it. Then, if you make it, they'll be against you staying there."

Gary considered what Evan Walker was saying. He took it seriously, because Walker was the first person he'd ever met who knew what he was talking about. "You just heard our record," Gary said. "Do you think we should forget it?"

"Oh, no." Walker laughed. "If I did that I'd run the risk of being known as the disc jockey who told"—he leaned over and looked at the label on the band's single—"who told the Electric Outlet they'd never make it. I think your music shows promise, especially for a group so young. But, remember, boys, just because I play a record on the radio doesn't mean you're going to be one of those two hundred bands that someday makes it for a few months or even a few years. Whether or not a record company thinks you can make money is a whole different story."

Inside, Gary wasn't certain what all this meant, but somehow he knew he should be feeling very happy. Meanwhile, Evan Walker was looking at his watch. "You need those?" he said, pointing to a few copies of the band's single that Gary was still holding. Gary shook his head. "Okay, leave 'em here," Evan Walker said.

Gary and Karl looked at each other.

"You mean, you're going to play *our record* on the radio?" Karl asked.

Evan Walker smiled. "Tell your friends to listen to the show tonight," he said.

Seventeen

Karl said he couldn't stay up late to listen to Walker's show because he had to go to work the next morning. Susan said she was going out with Michael. Oscar said he'd heard the songs enough already—he didn't see why he should stay up all night just to hear them again. So Gary knew he'd be staying up that night alone.

He thought about calling some of his friends from school, but decided against it. He didn't really have many close friends outside of the band anymore—maybe one or two guys he messed around with in the music room at school and a few who played basketball. He'd never really thought about it before, but now it occurred to him that in his freshman and sophomore years he'd had a lot of friends. What had happened?

The band had happened. Instead of hanging out with friends after school, he practiced guitar or rehearsed with the band or worked on songs with Oscar. Friday nights they either rehearsed or had a gig. And Saturday nights too. But how many Saturday nights had he just spent sitting in front of the tube because he'd been too busy all week with music to make plans with anyone? A lot.

And a lot of old friends had sort of faded away. He just couldn't see calling them now and telling them his band was going to be on the radio that night. Too much time had passed. What if he called and one of them said, "So what?"

It grew late and Gary sat on the floor of the Shrine, leaning against his bed. He played soft, tinny riffs on his acoustic guitar and thought about the things Evan Walker had said. The higher you go, the harder you fall. He chuckled. The thing about the Electric Outlet was, they were still so low that it didn't matter.

He wondered how many people would be listening at four in the morning when the Outlet's songs would probably get played. Two hundred? And of those two hundred, Gary was reasonably certain that 150 would be so stoned they wouldn't even remember the next morning what they'd heard.

And he knew that if the songs did get played he'd spend the weekend trekking back to all the rock clubs with copies of the band's single, telling the club owners or managers or anyone who would listen that Evan Walker had played the record on his show. With luck the band might land a few gigs. But Gary already knew from the Rock Garden and from what Walker said that the clubs were like the record companies. They didn't want to know how good your music was, they wanted to know how much money you could bring in. No wonder one of the biggest clubs in the city was called the Bottom Line. Because in business, the bottom line was always money.

Around one o'clock in the morning there was a light tap on his door and it opened enough for brother Thomas to stick his head in. The two brothers stared at each other for a second.

"What do you want?" Gary asked.

"You waiting for them to play your record?" Thomas asked back.

"Yeah."

"Can I wait too?"

"Uh, sure." Gary was a little surprised. Here was an unexpected visitor. Thomas Specter came into the room and sat down in the chair at Gary's desk. It had been quite a while since the two brothers had voluntarily sat alone in the same room together.

Thomas looked around and pointed to the walls and ceiling. "What's all that stuff?" he asked.

"Egg crates," Gary replied. "It's a way of sound-proofing. I put it up so I could play music late at night without disturbing anyone."

Thomas nodded. "Mind if I have a smoke?" he asked.

Gary shrugged and watched his little brother pull a cigarette out of his pocket. He didn't even know Thomas smoked. Gary got up and turned the air conditioner in his window to FAN-OPEN. "You better sit here," he told Thomas. "Blow the smoke into the vent or Mom will smell it."

Thomas moved his chair over and held the cigarette next to the vent. "All your friends gonna listen?" he asked.

"Uh, yeah," Gary said. All six million of them.

"Just about every kid I told said he was gonna listen," Thomas said, taking a puff of the cigarette. Gary noticed that his brother held the smoke in his mouth and then let it out in a tiny stream. He didn't inhale. "That reminds me." Thomas dug into his pocket and pulled out two crumpled bills and handed them to Gary. "Sold two more records today. And there are three kids who still owe me."

Gary took the money. That made something like twenty-two records his brother had sold so far.

"They gonna say your name over the air?" Thomas asked.

"I don't know," Gary said. "They may only mention the band."

"That's cool," Thomas said.

It was still too early to turn on the radio, so Gary just kept playing the guitar. Thomas watched. After a while he asked, "Is it hard to learn?"

"Naw, look." Gary handed the guitar to his brother. Thomas sat with the instrument in his lap, sliding his hand up and down the guitar's neck. A couple of times he tried to strum with the pick Gary had given him, but the results were hardly musical.

He looked up at Gary. "What do you do?"

"Here." Gary took his brother's fingers and positioned them at the end of the neck in a simple E chord. He let Thomas strum that for a while and then showed him a simple A chord. When Thomas had gotten used to both, he had him switch back and forth.

"Hey," Thomas said excitedly, "that sounds like music!"

"All you have to learn is one more chord and you'll be able to play eighty percent of all the rock songs ever written," Gary told him.

"Show me," Thomas said.

But Gary held back. "I thought you hated rock and roll."

"I like all kinds of music," Thomas said.

"Since when?" Gary asked.

Thomas grinned at him. "Since my brother became famous."

By the time the Evan Walker show began, Thomas had learned the D chord and Gary had shown him how to play two old Rolling Stones songs. Thomas's fingers kept getting mixed up at the chord changes, but it was still amazing how fast he was catching on. "Maybe I can play with your band," Thomas said eagerly.

Gary smiled. "Maybe."

It was time for the show, so they put away the guitar and turned on the radio. For the next hour Gary and Thomas listened for, but did not hear, the Electric Outlet's songs. Evan Walker didn't even mention the fact that he was going to play a new group that night. By 3:30 Thomas was having trouble keeping his eyes open and by 4:00 A.M. he was sprawled on Gary's bed, sound asleep. Gary himself was fighting not to nod off. He had to stay up. For all he knew he was the only person in New York listening to Evan Walker, and this might be the only time the record was ever played.

At a quarter to five it occurred to Gary that Evan Walker might not play his single. Maybe Evan Walker had forgotten who he was. No one out there, except a couple of Thomas's friends (if they were still awake), wanted to hear the songs anyway. Only about thirty people in the world even knew that the record existed. Gary wondered if this was just another broken promise. After all, no one really needed Gary Specter or the Electric Outlet. There were ten thousand other bands ready and willing to make it big. Even if a band as well known as Sold Out disappeared, there were a hundred bands to replace it.

"Sometimes I wonder who's listening at this

time of the morning." Across the room, Evan Walker's voice drifted out of the radio. Gary was sitting on the floor, his arms crossed over his knees and his head resting heavily on them. He was falling asleep. "But there's at least one person listening right now. And these next two songs are by his group, the Electric Outlet." Suddenly Gary was wide awake. Evan Walker was still talking. "The group is unsigned, unknown, and, you might think, unexceptional. But listen closely and you may think differently. And remember that no one in the group is older than seventeen. I advise you to pay attention to the lyrics. Also to the guitar solo in the first song. Remember, these are seventeen-year-olds. Also, you might note the opening and close of the second song. The music was written by a sixteen-year-old."

The next thing Gary knew, "Rock Therapy" was bopping out of the radio at him. It was unbelievable. Gary slapped himself on the face to make sure he was awake. Then he turned the radio dial off WHAT and then back on to make sure it was really real. It was! The song was still there! Gary heard *himself* singing on the radio. He heard his own guitar. It was too unbelievable to believe, too unreal to be real, too incredible to be credible.

But it happened. First "Rock Therapy," then "Educated Fool." Then Evan Walker was saying something about playing these songs again in a few nights and wanting some listener response, but Gary was too confused and excited to listen closely. He realized he'd forgotten to wake Thomas up. He looked at his brother, curled up on the bed covers, and decided against it. There was no reason to wake him now. For a few moments, Gary stood in the middle of the room not knowing what to do. It seemed to him like something big should happen the first time your songs were played on the radio, but standing there Gary realized that nothing was different. He was still Gary Specter, the band was still the unknown Electric Outlet. One play on the radio didn't change anything—the thought quickly sobered Gary up. Like Walter Sloves had said, they still had a long way to go. After a while, Gary lay down on the floor. Sleep was catching up fast, and he rolled up a pair of jeans to use for a pillow. As he closed his eyes he thought of the roulette wheel. Was it really worth it? The chances were so great against their making it. He remembered reading in a rock magazine that even for a big star like Bob Seger it took fifteen years to be discovered. And yet it seemed like he had no choice. If there was one thing Gary now knew for certain, it was that he had the fever. And Rock Therapy was the only cure.

Eighteen

It's hard to look for a dumb summer job as a stock boy in a supermarket when you think you're on the verge of rock stardom. The day after Evan Walker played the Electric Outlet's single on the radio, Gary tried two local supermarkets, learned that there were no jobs available, and decided he'd done enough job hunting for the day. Besides, he had to go down to Julio's music shop to buy new strings for his guitar.

Julio's was one of a bunch of music stores on 48th Street that were always crowded with young musicians. Many came just to hang out and talk about music and technical stuff like the kinds of guitars and amps they preferred and whether or not they were using a phaser or distortion that week. Of all the stores on 48th Street, Gary liked Julio's the best because the guys who worked there were also musicians and they didn't care if you just hung around all day and didn't buy a thing. At Julio's you could learn pretty quickly what hardware the big groups were using and who the current hot acts were. And sometimes a semifamous rock star would even stop in, supposedly to buy something, but mostly just to bask in the adoration and envy of all the other struggling musicians there who were still trying to get an act together.

As Gary stepped into the crowded, noisy music store that afternoon, he knew that he too had ulterior motives. Suppose, for instance, someone happened to be raving about this incredible new band Evan Walker had played on the radio the night before. Gary might just have to admit that he was the lead singer and guitarist of the group.

Julio's was packed with musicians trying equipment, or talking to the salesmen, or just hanging around. Toward the back of the store, past the long rows of guitars chained to racks so they couldn't be stolen, Gary saw a crowd of kids and knew instantly that someone at least quasi-important was there. Curious, he made his way toward the crowd. Most of the kids were younger —closer to Thomas's age—and Gary had no trouble peeking over their heads at the object of their interest. There, in a corner, a musician with shoulder-length brown hair and wearing a brightly colored Hawaiian shirt was plugging a guitar into an amp.

"Hey, Johnny," someone in the crowd yelled, and Johnny Fantasy of the Zoomies looked up from the amp. Gary's heart beat like a drumstick on a snare drum.

"Where are you playing next?" someone else asked him.

You could see that Johnny Fantasy was a real showman. Instead of answering right away, he waited until the crowd grew quiet, eager for his answer. Then he said, "We're opening for the Usual Suspects at the Palladium in two weeks."

All around him Gary heard gasps. "Oh, wow!" "You hear that!" "Unreal!" The Palladium was a full-sized concert hall that booked everyone except the biggest superstar acts. The Usual Suspects were a British band who had about five albums out and were on the radio all the time. Gary knew that getting to be their opening act automatically elevated the Zoomies from just being a good local band to minor deity level.

Johnny Fantasy turned up the volume on the amp and ran through a couple of uncomplicated riffs—nothing Gary or half a dozen other guitarists in the store couldn't do. Gary noticed that none of the older musicians in the store were paying much attention to him. A few might stop near the back of the crowd and listen to Johnny's riffs for a moment, but then they'd smirk and walk away, leaving Johnny with his crowd of groupies.

Meanwhile, one of Julio's salesmen hovered nearby. Johnny might have been there to buy a new guitar or amp, or maybe he just felt like showing off. Either way, he was playing with a guitar that was easily worth a thousand bucks and someone from the store had to watch him to make sure he didn't drop it or just walk off with it "by accident."

Someone else in the crowd asked Johnny who his favorite guitarist was. Johnny looked at the kid with a sly grin on his face and said, "Me." And then, as if to accentuate the point, he played another, longer riff. In degree of difficulty, Gary gave it a 3.5 on a scale of ten.

More questions were asked, and Johnny responded with more answers and more riffs. You could tell that the kids were really impressed with Johnny, but no one seemed more impressed than Johnny himself. Gary was starting to get turned off by the guy's absolute conceit. After all, there were a *few* other bands in the world besides the Zoomies.

"Hey," someone yelled, "when are you guys gonna come out with another single?" So far the Zoomies had produced three or four singles on their own. But an album contract with one of the big record companies still eluded them.

"We're working on one right now," Johnny answered. "The Zoomies fan club gets almost a hundred letters a week begging us for a new record. So we gotta do it."

"Outa sight," someone said, and several others concurred, but Gary had the feeling that some other musicians in the store were getting ticked off by Johnny's attitude. After all, who really cared about fan clubs? Johnny played another short riff on the guitar and then waited to field another question. It was like some kind of news conference for the benefit of his ego.

Just then an older guy, closer to Johnny's and Gary's age, walked up to the crowd with a couple of his friends. "Hey, Johnny," the guy yelled, "when are you gonna sign with a *real* record company?"

His friends laughed and Johnny Fantasy winced slightly. "Soon, man, soon," he mumbled, and started to play another riff, but it was obvious the news conference was ending. Even the groupies seemed to have had enough of Johnny's ego, and they were starting to split. In the middle of the riff Johnny abruptly stopped playing and got up to leave.

The salesman who'd been hovering over him reached to take the expensive guitar back. "How'd you like it?" he asked.

Johnny looked at the salesman distastefully. "The action sucks," he said, and started out of the store.

On impulse, Gary followed him out to the street. It was weird how the Zoomie had gone from being the center of attention to being an outcast so fast. You really had to be careful about what you said to people or you could turn them off no matter who you were, Gary thought. He let Johnny get a safe distance ahead of him down the sidewalk before he followed, curious to see where he'd go. After all, Johnny Fantasy was still Johnny Fantasy—even if he was a flaming egomaniac.

Staying about fifty feet behind him, Gary followed Johnny for several blocks. The Zoomie didn't do anything too much out of the ordinary, except that every time he saw a pretty girl approaching he'd automatically adjust his path so that he'd be heading straight at her. A few girls smiled at him and a few gave him funny looks, but all managed to get off the collision course and keep going. Gary guessed that Johnny was hoping one of them might recognize him.

About a block later Johnny passed a record store and stopped to look into the display window. He stood there for a long time and Gary had to smile. This time he was almost certain he knew what Johnny was doing—picturing himself and the Zoomies on the covers of the albums inside. It was something Gary did all the time. Geez, he thought, even Johnny Fantasy, who had four singles and who was going to open for the Usual Suspects at the Palladium, does it.

After a while the guitarist moved on, this time walking more quickly. Gary almost had to jog to keep up with him. Suddenly, he turned a corner and Johnny Fantasy was gone. Gary quickly looked up and down the street, but there was no sign of the Zoomie. It was impossible that Johnny could have disappeared so fast, unless . . . Near the corner was a subway station. Gary stood at the entrance. Maybe Johnny Fantasy didn't take limos, as Gary had imagined. Maybe he didn't even take taxis. The Zoomies might be playing the Palladium in a few weeks, they might even be going on tour the following fall, and maybe someday they'd be a big supergroup like Sold Out. But right now Johnny Fantasy was just another kid on the subway. Knowing that somehow made Gary feel better.

Nineteen

Susan's friend Michael, the associate publicity guy from Columbia Records, had given her four backstage passes to a Deranged concert at the Wollman skating rink in Central Park. Of all the weirdo, crazy groups around, Deranged was, well, the most deranged. They performed in Halloween ghost and goblin costumes and did stuff like kill live chickens on stage, shoot fire extinguishers at the audience, set off all kinds of fireworks, and destroy all sorts of things, including their instruments. In Cleveland, Gary had read, they'd dressed in Tarzan outfits and swung onto the stage with ropes hung from the ceiling of the theater. In Austin, Texas, they'd driven an old Cadillac on stage and smashed it with sledgehammers. In Miami, it was rumored, the drummer had played an entire concert without any pants on. Gary had heard that the band was so notorious that they had to post a $50,000 bond at every hotel they stayed at to cover any damage they might do. Most serious musicians didn't have much respect for Deranged since they weren't really a band— they were more like a musical demolition derby.

Still, being backstage for a concert, a major concert, would be a gas, and on the day of the Deranged concert Gary was really excited. Early that evening he and Susan waited for Karl and Oscar at the police barrier near the backstage entrance. Even though the concert was not due to begin for another hour, the grounds near the skating rink were crowded with hundreds of kids milling around, while thousands more stood on line waiting to be let in for the show. As Gary and Susan watched, some pleaded with cops to let them sneak past the barrier to get a look at the stage. Others tried to climb the scaffolding that supported the stage and were chased away by the police. At least once a minute a different long-haired, weird-looking character would come up to Gary and ask if he had any tickets to sell. Oddly, some of the strangest-looking ones—like a guy wearing ripped jeans and a T-shirt that looked like it had been through a paper shredder—offered the most money. Gary refused all offers.

Now a big greasy-looking guy with a red bandana wrapped around his forehead and a torn Deranged T-shirt on approached them.

"Hey, got any extra tickets?" he asked. He looked big enough to be a professional football player, Gary thought nervously as he shook his head. The brute gave Susan the hairy eyeball. "Hey, doll," he leered, "you waitin' to go backstage? You a girl friend of the band's?"

"Get lost," Susan said sharply.

The big guy grinned. "I wouldn't mind gettin' lost with you, doll."

Gary stepped close to the guy. "Hey, listen, another guy just walked by here saying he had some tickets to sell." Gary pointed eastward. "He went that way."

The brute's eyes lit up. "Hey, thanks," he said, heading eastward.

Susan smiled. "Thanks, cuz," she said. Gary had noticed that she'd been in a pensive mood all day. She'd certainly gotten dressed up nicely— her hair was braided in the front and she was wearing lipstick and eye shadow and a pretty green blouse and tight jeans. She was even wearing her favorite pair of purple cowboy boots, which Gary knew she saved for special occasions. He wondered why she was so solemn.

"Hey, what's wrong?" he asked.

Susan shrugged.

"You should be excited," Gary said. "We're going backstage."

Susan smiled the same sad smile she'd had all day. "I wish my parents would come back from Australia," she said wistfully. "At least, I wish Mom would."

"How come?"

"I miss her," Susan said. "I don't have anyone to talk to."

"What about my mom?" Gary asked.

"Are you kidding?" Susan said with half a laugh.

"Well, what's wrong?" Gary asked. "Want to tell me?"

Susan looked at him for a long moment without speaking. It seemed as if part of her wanted to tell him and part didn't.

"I promise I won't tell anyone," Gary said.

Susan nodded. "I don't think Michael likes me anymore," she said.

"Why? He gave you these tickets, didn't he?"

"It's just a feeling." Susan sighed. "He says I'm too serious."

"Are you?"

"I don't know," Susan said, heavyhearted. Gary watched as she carefully wiped some water from her eye so it wouldn't mess up her mascara.

Oscar arrived. "I can't believe you talked me into going to this ridiculous concert," he said, looking at the crowd with scorn in his eyes.

"I don't recall having to talk you into it," Gary said. Meanwhile, he noticed that Susan had started sniffing the air. Gary took a deep breath. The air did smell strange—sort of sweet, almost like . . .

"Roses," Susan said, looking around. Gary also looked around. The smell of roses was growing so strong that he was certain a florist must have just delivered several large bouquets to the stage. Maybe Deranged was planning to use them in their act that night. But there were no roses, there was only . . .

"Oscar?" Susan said.

"You'll get used to it," Oscar said quickly. "In a few moments you won't even smell a thing."

"In your hair?" Gary asked incredulously.

"Just forget it, okay?" Oscar snapped. "You won't even notice it in a second."

But the smell of roses around them seemed to get stronger and stronger until Gary started to feel a little ill. "I hope that stuff is good for your hair," he said, gagging, "because it's murder on my nose."

"It's a special formula of concentrated rose hip cream and it's very, very expensive, so don't ask me to wash it off," Oscar said. "It comes from South America. You can't even buy it in the United States."

"Thank God." Susan was trying to fan some fresh air toward her face.

"Well, it's going to save my hair," Oscar insisted.

"Yeah, but who's going to save our noses?" Gary asked, pinching his nostrils closed.

At that moment Karl rode up on the old bicycle he sometimes used to deliver messages. Over his shoulder was the bright orange delivery bag. He looked breathless. "Has anyone been listening to Walker's show the last couple of nights?" he gasped.

They shook their heads. No one could stay up that late every night.

Karl began to say something, but stopped and sniffed instead. "Hey, what's that smell?"

"The squirrels are in heat," Susan said.

Karl crinkled up his nose. "The squirrels?"

"Forget it," Gary said. "What about the radio?"

"Walker's been playing our songs every night," Karl said. "Last night my mom couldn't sleep and she listened. She said he even got a request for 'Educated Fool.' "

The members of the band gawked at him.

"And listen to this," Karl said. "On the way up here I stopped at Bleecker Joe's to see how the single is selling. Joe went nuts when he found out who I was. He said he's been trying to find us for a week. Turns out whenever Evan Walker features a local group, Bleecker Joe does a window display of the record in his shop. Sort of a tie-in or something. He wants a hundred copies of our record."

Gary suddenly recalled something. "Remember when Walker featured the Zoomies—they had a full window at Bleecker Joe's. We should have gone down there the day Walker started playing us."

"And he wants a poster of the band to go with the display," Karl said.

This was great, except they didn't have a poster. Meanwhile, Karl had started sniffing again and each sniff brought him closer to Oscar's head.

"Hey!" Oscar yelled. "Keep your nose to yourself."

"Ah-ha!" Karl said, nodding wisely.

"What about your mom?" Gary asked Karl.

"She doesn't smell that bad," Karl said.

"No, I mean, she's got some pictures of the band," Gary said. "Could she get one blown up poster size?"

"I guess," he said, "if we pay her back."

"Great," said Gary. "Tell her to try and get a poster over to Bleecker Joe's as fast as possible."

The long line of ticket holders had started to move into the rink and Gary suggested that they go backstage, but just then a man appeared near them, asking if anyone had any backstage passes for sale. He was wearing a pair of designer jeans and a chambray shirt open to his belly button, revealing lots of curly brown chest hair and at least half a dozen long gold chains. With him was a blond woman who was also wearing designer jeans and a white blouse open to her belly button —practically.

"How much?" Karl asked.

The man walked over, followed by the blond woman. "Got a pair?" he asked. Gary noticed the man's teeth were perfectly white. Too white— they were capped.

"Maybe," Karl said.

"Give ya fifty for the pair," the man said.

Karl shook his head.

"Seventy?" the man asked. "That's thirty-five bucks apiece."

Gary couldn't believe it. For $35 he'd gladly sell his backstage pass. But Karl shook his head again. "Hundred for the pair," he said.

The man frowned and looked at the blond woman, who shrugged. The next thing Gary knew, the man was reaching into his pocket and pulling out a wad of bills. "What the hell," he grumbled. "It's only money."

Meanwhile, Karl was looking around at the rest of the band. One of them had to give up a pass to make the pair. Gary glanced at Susan, but she said, "I want to go in. Michael's going to be there. Please come with me, Gary."

Everyone looked at Oscar.

"What's that funny smell?" the man with the gold chains asked.

"Come on, Oscar," Karl hissed. "It's fifty bucks apiece."

Oscar looked around at everyone. "I want sixty for mine," he said. The man with a gold chains shook his head.

"Don't be greedy," Karl said. "They probably won't let you in smelling like that anyway."

Oscar looked incensed. For a moment Gary thought he was going to march through the backstage entrance just to prove that they would let him in, but then he acquiesced. "I wouldn't want to go to a concert with you anyway," he said to Karl, giving up his pass to the man and taking his money. He bade farewell to Gary and Susan and left. The belly-button people got their passes and went in.

Karl got back on his bike. "Easiest fifty bucks I ever made," he said happily.

"What are you going to do with it?" Susan asked.

"I'm gonna get some incredible, er . . ." Karl looked at Gary and Susan and grinned sheepishly. "I'm gonna get some incredible interest on it in my bank account," he said, and pedaled off.

Gary and Susan showed their passes to the policeman at the backstage entrance and were allowed in. Backstage was crowded with all sorts of people. Right down the middle was a long table loaded from one end to the other with cold cuts and bottles of everything from Perrier to Scotch to Coke. The funny thing was, the only people who were eating the stuff were the belly-button people. As Gary and Susan passed them, Gary said hello, but they pretended not to know who he was. Gary looked around, but didn't see anyone in costumes who resembled Deranged. He figured the band probably waited until the fans were all inside the rink before they arrived. Otherwise they'd get mobbed.

Suddenly Susan sprinted across the room and threw her arms around a short guy in a beige suit with a big bush of curly brown hair on his head.

The guy had been talking to some other people, and he seemed a little embarrassed as Susan hugged him. Gary walked across the room and arrived just as Susan let go. "Gary," she said, still keeping one arm around the guy's waist, "this is Michael."

Michael held out his hand and Gary shook it. "Good to meet you, Gary," the associate publicity director said. "I've heard a lot about you."

"Same here," Gary said.

"So how's the band doing?" Michael asked him.

"Great," Gary told him. "We just heard that Evan Walker's been playing our record every night."

Michael looked surprised. "Hey, that's super." Then he turned to Susan. "I keep asking you to let me hear it."

"I, uh, didn't think you really cared," Susan said.

Michael turned back to Gary. "Well, I would like to hear it, Gary."

"Sure," Gary said. "I'll get you a copy." He hated to admit it but he could sense that Michael was a likeable guy and not the creep he had imagined he'd be.

It turned out to be a great night for Gary. He learned a lot about the rock-and-roll business, especially from Michael. Even though Michael admitted that the big record companies didn't take high school bands very seriously, he talked to Gary like he was a serious musician and told him what the band could do to make it big. The first and foremost rule was, "Stay together." As they talked, Michael tried to be nice to Susan, but Gary could see that he was annoyed by the way she clung to him. For the first time in a long while, Gary saw Susan acting like the teenager she really was. She had a real crush on Michael. Unfortunately it was obvious to Gary that the publicity director was trying to cool things off.

Then Deranged arrived and Gary forgot all about his cousin's love problems. Deranged was a real shock. Instead of the four crazed maniacs who assaulted sound stages in strange costumes, destroying everything in sight, the four musicians who stood around backstage and chatted while waiting for the opening act to end were just normal, nice guys from Norfolk, Virginia. Gary even got introduced (by Michael) to two of them, and when he confessed that they didn't seem anything like the crazies he'd seen on late-night TV rock concerts, they laughed. "There's an old show-biz saying," one of them said with a southern accent, "that you got to give the people what they want."

Then Gary, Susan, Michael, and everyone else stood backstage while those four nice guys transformed themselves into Deranged. By the end of the night they'd set off dozens of smoke bombs, thrown water balloons at the audience, lit an amp on fire, smashed another on the stage floor, destroyed their guitars with a chain saw, and, in what must have been a planned finale, were handcuffed and led from the stage by four New York City policemen. At the end of the act Gary couldn't remember the melody of a single song they'd played, but he had to admit they'd put on one hell of a show.

With the concert over, Susan wanted Michael and Gary to go out with her and it was hard to believe Michael when he said he had to run back to his office to take care of some work. As they said good-bye on a street corner near the park, Michael kept glancing at Gary as if to say, "I'm sorry I caused this mess." Finally he turned and walked away in the dark, leaving Gary alone with his obviously unhappy cousin.

For a while they walked in the dark and said nothing. Gary felt bad for Susan, but at least in one respect he was glad—glad to know that she was still a teenager like the rest of the band. She might have dressed fancier, acted more mature, and gone out with older guys, but when it came right down to it, seventeen was seventeen, not twenty-one, not twenty-five.

"I wish I knew what I was doing wrong," Susan said sadly.

"Maybe you're not doing anything wrong," Gary said. "Maybe you're just a little too young for him right now."

"But that's not my fault," Susan argued.

"No, but sometimes it's just the way things are. You can't make yourself older and he can't make himself younger."

"So why can't we remain the ages we are?" Susan asked. She was really upset.

Gary put his arm around her shoulder. "You know how he was telling me that record companies don't take high school bands seriously?" he asked, hugging her.

"Uh-huh."

"Well, I have a feeling that goes for high schoolers in general."

Thanks to Karl's mother, the Electric Outlet took another step toward big time. She got them their first interview—in a thin underground newspaper called *New York Scenes*. It wasn't *Rolling Stone*, but it was a start.

The day of the interview the Electric Outlet met outside Bleecker Joe's. They were supposed to be interviewed at Karl's apartment a few blocks away, but the band had agreed to meet at the record store first to look at their record display. They'd all seen it before, but still, it couldn't hurt to take one more look.

Karl was waiting outside the record shop when Gary got there. With him was a tall, awkward girl with dirty-blond hair whose name was Randy. She'd been with Karl a lot lately. Gary didn't know her very well—she hardly ever spoke—but she seemed nice, and she even had some acne to go along with Karl's.

Oscar and Susan soon arrived and, together with Randy, the band gazed through Bleecker Joe's window at the big black-and-white poster made from a photo Mrs. Roesch had taken one night at the Rock Garden. You could see Gary in his straitjacket with Susan to his left, her hair flying, and Oscar to the right, hunched over the keyboard on top of the ironing board. Unfortunately, the way Oscar was bent over you could see his ever-progressing baldness through the thin hair on the top of his head. And all you could see of Karl behind Gary, Susan, and the drum set were two long arms flailing.

Gary looked at his watch. "Guess we better get over to your mother's," he said to Karl.

"No, wait," Karl said, still staring at the poster of the band and the copies of their single in the window. "I'm enjoying this."

"Does it bother you that we can't see your face in the poster?" Randy asked him.

"Are you kidding?" Karl said. "That's what I like about it."

Oscar stood tight-lipped as usual.

"What do you think?" Gary asked.

"I think I'm going to start wearing a hat," Oscar said.

"I think bald men are sexy, Oscar," Susan said.

Oscar pouted. "That must be why so many girls call me, begging for dates," he said sarcastically.

Just then a kid wearing a green Army surplus jacket walked out of Bleecker Joe's. He glanced into the window to see what the band was looking at, then stopped abruptly. "Hey," he said, astonished. "You guys are those guys." He pointed at the poster.

Karl nodded.

"Oh, wow," the kid said, staring at the band with his mouth open. Gary felt kind of funny. "Oh, wow," the kid said again. Susan glanced at Gary. She looked like she was holding back the giggles.

Finally, Gary held out his hand. "Uh, my name's Gary Specter and this is the Electric Outlet."

The kid looked at Gary's hand as if he didn't know what to do with it. Then he quickly grabbed it and shook. "Hey, wow, you guys are for real." The kid kept shaking Gary's hand.

"Yes, we are real," Oscar said.

"Uh, hey, don't go anywhere." The kid disappeared back into the store.

"Our first fan," Susan said.

"I thought my mother was our first fan," said Karl.

"Our first unrelated fan," Gary said.

A second later the kid was back, pressing a copy of their single toward them. "Could you autograph it?" he asked.

"Uh, sure," Gary said, but he searched his pockets and couldn't find a pen. Neither could Susan, Karl, Randy, or Oscar.

The kid disappeared into the shop again and quickly returned with a pen. "Would you write 'To Jerry' on it?" he asked.

"Sure." The four members of the Electric Outlet took turns signing the record jacket. Jerry uttered several more "Oh, wows" and then thanked them and left. The four band members watched him go.

"Rule number one for success," Susan said. "Always carry a pen."

•

Karl's apartment was pretty small, especially for two people. There was one bedroom where Mrs. Roesch slept, while Karl had to sleep on a convertible couch in the living room. Gary supposed it must have been a drag having no privacy, but Karl had never had his own bedroom, so it probably didn't matter.

Gary had never really paid close attention to Mrs. Roesch before. He used to think she was kind of flaky—a mother who was a groupie to her son's rock band. But he was impressed with how she'd handled the arrangements for the Pin Club, and how she'd gotten Evan Walker to see them, and how she'd made the poster and gotten them this interview. He didn't mind that she was beginning to take charge of the business end of the group. In fact, it was a relief to Gary, since she seemed to know what to do when he didn't. As they entered the apartment, he saw that she'd straightened the place up and put out crackers and cheese.

It was the first time Susan and Oscar had been in Karl's apartment, and Susan went to look at some framed posters on the wall. Some of them showed peace symbols or graphics of angry demonstrators; others announced marches against the war in Vietnam or for civil rights in the South. Susan joined the rest of the band around the coffee table. "We studied some of that stuff in history last year," she told Mrs. Roesch.

Karl's mother shook her head. "Don't tell me about it. I don't want to know that I'm that old." Then she asked if anyone wanted beer or wine. Gary breathed a sigh of relief. If the interview had been done at his house, his mother would have offered Coke or ginger ale. He could just see the interviewer writing that up—"The Electric Outlet is a fairly young band. Their idea of refreshments is Coca-Cola and potato chips."

They sat around the table. Karl and Gary had beer, Susan, Mrs. Roesch, and Randy had white wine, and Oscar had a 7-Up. But at least it looked clear, like Perrier, and the interviewer would never know.

"Nervous?" Mrs. Roesch asked.

"About what?" Karl asked.

"Your first interview," his mother said.

"Naw."

"What are you going to say?" Mrs. Roesch asked.

"Mom, we're just gonna answer the questions," Karl said irritably. Gary knew that Karl got annoyed when his mother stuck her nose into the band's business. But, after all, she was their manager and she'd done a good job so far.

"Wait, Karl," Gary said. "I think we should listen to your mom."

"Oh, come on, Gary, we can do it ourselves," Karl said.

"No, I agree with Gary," Susan said. She turned to Mrs. Roesch. "I think you're right. There may be things we want the interviewer to know. Or things we don't."

"Like what?" Oscar asked.

"Well, I think the most important thing is to try to agree on the image you want the band to present," Karl's mother said. "You want to be recognizable so that they'll remember you."

"Aw, bull," Karl said.

"A lot of bands do have an image," Gary said. "I mean, you gotta have music. But people need something more than that, too. They want something they can identify with."

"But that's artificial," Oscar argued. "Our image should be in our music."

"But it isn't, Oscar," Susan said. "Look at Blondie. They're all capable musicians, but their image is Deborah Harry. You don't make something up, but you take something in the band and build on it."

"Yeah," said Gary. "You know what the Beatles originally made it on? It wasn't just the screaming music. It was the hair. They were the original longhairs."

"If you don't count Mozart," Oscar said.

"And the Stones," Gary said. "I read that they purposely tried to look like bad guys, and the Grateful Dead made it with acid rock. I'm not saying we have to be another Deranged, but look at the Zoomies—they've developed their own pop image. What do we have?"

They all looked at each other. What exactly did they have?

"Well, we have Gary," Susan said.

"Yes," said Mrs. Roesch. "And since he's the front man and leader of the group, I think your new name should start with Gary Specter."

"Our new name?" Karl asked.

"Are any of you particularly attached to the Electric Outlet?" his mother asked.

No one said anything.

"Gary Specter and what?" Oscar asked.

"How about Gary Specter and the Divorce Rate?" Susan said.

"How about Gary Specter and the Gross National Product?" Gary asked.

"Dumb," said Oscar.

"Gary Specter and the Growing Pains?"

"You are a growing pain."

"Jim Suit and the Volleyballs?"

"What does that have to do with anything?"

"I don't know, it just sounds neat."

"Hooky and De Tensions?"

"Ha ha."

"Last Minute and the All-Nite Crammers?"

"What?"

"First Period and the Curses?"

"Gross."

"But funny."

"Stop," Mrs. Roesch said. "You have to decide on something and you don't have much time."

"I like Gross National Product," Gary said.

"I like Divorce Rate," said Susan.

"How about Gary Specter and the Coming Attractions?" Randy asked.

"Hey, I like that!" Karl said.

"I don't like any of them," Oscar said.

"All right, wait," Mrs. Roesch said. She got up and went into the kitchen. A moment later she was back with four straws sticking out of her hand. "Each of you pick a straw," she told them. "The longest one wins."

Gary, Susan, Oscar, and Karl each picked a straw. Karl's was the longest.

"So it's Gary Specter and the Coming Attractions."

"Okay," Gary said. "I'll accept it for now." He looked at Oscar. "What do you think?"

"It's not fair," Oscar grumbled.

186 • Todd Strasser

"What isn't fair?" Karl asked.

Oscar looked at them unhappily. "I write all the music. Why should Gary get all the credit?"

Gary nodded. "He's right. Without Oscar we wouldn't be us."

"What would you suggest?" Mrs. Roesch asked Oscar.

"How about Oscar Roginoff and the Coming Attractions," Oscar said.

Susan sighed. "Somehow it doesn't have the same ring to it."

"How about this," said Karl. "Gary Specter and the Coming Attractions Featuring Oscar Roginoff."

"That's better," Oscar said.

No one else seemed exactly thrilled. But just then the doorbell rang and everyone fell quiet. "That's the interviewer," Mrs. Roesch whispered, getting up.

"Any last-minute ideas?" Gary asked in a hushed voice.

Everyone shook their heads or shrugged.

"Then I guess we better stick with it," Gary said.

"Wait," Oscar hissed. "How about Oscar Roginoff and the Coming Attractions Featuring Gary Specter?" But Mrs. Roesch was already letting the interviewer from *New York Scenes* into the apartment.

The interviewer was a woman named Jean whose short hair was dyed pink and who wore skintight black pants and a weird leopard-skin blouse. The first thing she did in the apartment was take out a joint and ask the band if they minded if she got high. "I have to get myself in the *mood*," she stressed, "or I won't be able to *relate* to what it's like to be a struggling young band on the edge of fame."

Jean then proceeded to smoke the whole joint without even asking if any of them would care for a hit. Then the interview began, except it wasn't really an interview—at least not the way Gary had imagined his first interview would be. Jean spent most of the time telling the band about all the famous rock stars she'd interviewed and what "sexist pigs" and "egomaniacs" they all were. Gary asked her about the Zoomies and she said, "Oh, they're cute, but they'll never make it."

"Why not?" Karl asked.

"Have you seen them lately?" Jean said. "They try too hard. They're trying so hard to make it and so hard to please the audience that they've completely lost their sense of music. They're so worried about their image that all they are is an image. There's no real band behind it."

Gary and the rest of the band looked nervously at each other.

Jean the interviewer took out another joint and lit it. "So, tell me who you are," she said.

"Uh, I'm Gary Specter, lead guitarist and singer," Gary said. Then he introduced Karl and

Susan. When he got to Oscar, he said, "This is our keyboard man and song composer. He's only sixteen, but he's a musical genius."

"And what's the name of your group?" Jean asked.

Gary was about to tell her, but Oscar quickly said, "Gary Specter and the Coming Attractions Featuring Oscar Roginoff, the sixteen-year-old musical genius."

Jean looked up from her note pad. "Isn't that a little long?" she asked.

"Yes," Mrs. Roesch said. "Just make it Gary Specter and the Coming Attractions Plus Oscar."

By the end of the following week the next issue of
New York Scenes had come out, but the interview with Gary Specter and the Coming Attractions
Plus Oscar wasn't in it. That was a letdown, but
considering how weird Jean the interviewer had
been, none of them was really surprised. In a
way the whole week had been a disappointment,
but Gary and the band had known it was coming.
Evan Walker was featuring a new band called
Pocket Size and the Calculators on his show.
Bleecker Joe had taken down the band's poster and
display now that Walker was no longer featuring
their songs. Gary told the rest of the band that
such letdowns must be part of the music business.
"After all," he said, "even the Beatles' record dis-
plays didn't stay up forever."

June was turning into July and the band was
starting to practice for the gig at Galaxy One, the

small club downtown that had booked the band months before. At first Gary had been tempted to cancel the Galaxy One date. Now that the Coming Attractions had been featured by Evan Walker and Bleecker Joe's he didn't want club owners to get the impression that they worked for free. But Mrs. Roesch convinced him that the Galaxy One date would be a good warm-up for the gigs she hoped the band's recent publicity would lead to. Mrs. Roesch was already talking to other club managers and some people at record companies, trying to persuade them to come down to Galaxy One to hear the band play. Gary was glad that she'd taken over the band's business concerns. With practicing, writing new songs, and just trying to keep the band together musically, he was busy enough.

Thomas was a real help, too. He'd given up roller-skating to become the band's first official roadie, helping them move equipment and set up every time they practiced, acting as a sound man, and telling them when someone was playing or singing too loudly or too softly. He even turned out to be a whiz at fixing stuff like broken guitar cords and amps.

One night in early July the band was in the rehearsal studio working on some new songs for the Galaxy One gig. Thomas had gone out to get cold drinks for the band members and now he rushed back into the rehearsal room waving something in his hand.

"It's the interview! Look!" he shouted.

The band stopped playing and quickly huddled around Thomas, who opened the newest issue of *New York Scenes* to a photo of the band Jean the interviewer had taken. The photo was out of focus and all they could see were four fuzzy-looking figures.

"Is that me?" Gary asked, pointing to one of the figures.

"No, I think that's the philodendron," Karl said.

"Hey, listen to this," Oscar said excitedly. " 'The source of the group's undeniably fresh funk sound is a sixteen-year-old musical genius, Oscar Roginoff!' " Oscar jumped up to his feet. "That's me!"

Meanwhile, Susan read aloud, " 'Despite the band's youth, they display a seriousness about their music that is often lacking in young groups today. One senses they work as hard on their music as others work on becoming famous.' "

"Incredible!"

"Amazing!"

"Keep reading, Susan."

Susan read: " 'Listening to their single, self-produced and (for the time being at least) only available at Bleecker Joe's, one senses that if there is any weakness in the band's music, it is . . .' "

Susan stopped reading. "Come on, Susan," Karl urged her. "What does it say?" But Susan let the paper drop to the floor and got up.

"What's with her?" Oscar asked, as Susan ran quickly from the room.

Thomas picked up the paper. " 'If there is any weakness in the band's music,' " he read, " 'it is in their bassist, Susan Specter, the only female member of the group. While she is certainly attractive and her presence on stage must enhance the band's image in this age of sexist rock and roll, her bass playing lacks the strength and urgency a funk band like the Coming Attractions needs.' "

Gary was already heading for the hallway to look for his cousin. He found her at the end of the hall, her face pressed into a corner as if she were trying to disappear into the wall.

"Susan?"

"Go away," she whispered.

"Susan, that lady doesn't know what she's talking about," Gary said. "You can't tell anything just from listening to the single. She's crazy, Susan."

Susan turned from the corner and looked at him with reddened eyes. She rubbed a few tears away with the palms of her hands. "It's not just that," she sniffed. "Michael told me last night he doesn't want to see me anymore."

"Oh." Gary didn't know what to say.

"And she *is* right, Gary," Susan said. "I'm not good enough for the band. I'm just a silly girl guys like to watch and play with." She started to cry again. "They don't take me seriously."

Gary put his arms around her and she pressed

her face against his shoulder. "I do, Susan. The band does. That's why we've been trying to get you to practice." Gary could feel his cousin's tears seep through his shirt. He patted her on the back. "You're our bass player and we want you to stay."

Susan wiped her eyes again and Gary let go of her. "Listen, Gary," she said. "I don't want to rehearse anymore tonight. I just want to go home. Will you tell the rest of the band for me?"

"Sure." He really didn't want her to leave—the band still needed to practice—but he understood that she wanted to be alone.

Susan kissed him on the cheek and walked quickly down the hall. Gary waited until she turned the corner and then went back to the rehearsal room.

"Where's Susan?" Karl asked.

Gary shrugged. "She went home. I gotta talk to her later."

"What are you going to do?" Oscar asked anxiously.

"I don't know, Oscar," Gary said. "You know how you complain that she isn't good enough for the band. Well, maybe we ought to find someone new."

Oscar looked at him uncertainly.

"Yeah, Oscar," Karl said. "You said she was the weakest part of the group."

"Well, I, uh, I wasn't serious," Oscar said. "I don't want her to go, really. Get her back, please?"

Karl and Gary looked at each other and smiled.

Then Karl said, "Here's something else you gotta read." He pointed to the paper.

GALAXY ONE: CENTER OF THE MUSIC UNIVERSE

In the music world, hot clubs come and go faster than the life cycle of a mayfly. This summer's indisputably hot new club in New York is Galaxy One at 141 Warren Street. Nick Lowe, Tom Petty, and Bruce "the Boss" Springsteen are regulars when they're in town and the club is drawing the hottest new acts. Note: club owner Sam Kline is sticking to new acts. "We're new and we want only new acts with us. That's our style," he says. What he doesn't mention is that new acts come cheap. But who cares, so long as the music is good?

"Unbelievable," Gary muttered.

"Better make sure they still want us," said Karl.

"I'll call them tomorrow," Gary said.

"What about Susan?" Thomas asked.

"If I have to get down on my knees and beg her to play, I will," Gary said.

Twenty-Two

That night Gary's mother looked worried.

"What is it?" Gary asked.

"Susan told me she isn't going out tonight," Mrs. Specter said.

"So? What are you worried about?" Gary said. "You should be relieved."

"But if she isn't going out, something must be wrong," his mother insisted. "Gary, go upstairs and make sure she's feeling all right, will you?"

Gary suppressed a laugh. "Sure, Mom," he said. "I was gonna go up there anyway."

As he climbed the stairs to his cousin's apartment, Gary heard the heavy thump of bass notes resonating through the walls. He had to knock loudly and finally shout through the door to get Susan's attention.

She opened the apartment door, holding the Fender bass in one hand. "Listen," she said before he could say anything. "You know that part in 'I Fell in Love with the Baby-sitter' where I usually play this one long note for the whole measure?" Susan played the note. "Well, I think I can play it like this." She played a quick series of notes. "Doesn't that sound peppier?"

"Uh, yeah, it does." Gary was confused.

"So then the whole bass line would sound like this," Susan said, and then played a much improved version of the bass for the song.

Gary nodded dumbly. After that afternoon he had been sure he was going to have to beg Susan to return to the band. Now it looked like he couldn't keep her away if he tried. "Uh, Susan, what about Michael?"

Susan stopped playing for a moment. "It was a silly teenage crush, Gary. Besides, he's too old for me."

"I see," Gary said. Talk about quick recoveries.

"By the way," Susan said, "I started working on a new song. Could you help me with it?"

"Uh, sure," Gary said. Susan put down the bass and went to get the work sheets for the song. It was a miraculous transformation from a few hours before, but Gary understood—it was Rock Therapy.

Karl's mother had a friend who ran a small printing shop in the Village and as a favor he made up three hundred posters for the Coming Attractions. It was the same picture of the band Mrs. Roesch had used for the Bleecker Joe display

except on the bottom it said, "Appearing July 17th
at Galaxy One."

Then, a week before the gig, Galaxy One ran
its usual advertisement in *The Village Voice*:

Appearing This Week
_____

TUESDAY

SLASHED
THE WHIP BOYS
And Special Guests:
LOW GRADE INFECTIONS

WEDNESDAY

ZOOMIES
RUPTURES
GARY SPECTER AND THE COMING
ATTRACTIONS PLUS OSCAR

THURSDAY

ALTERED EGOS

Gary was speechless. They were on the same
bill as the Zoomies!

Galaxy One ads also ran on the local rock
radio stations. That night Gary and Thomas
turned on every radio in the house and listened
to all the rock channels at once. Their band was
mentioned on three different stations. It was incredible—the Coming Attractions were in the
newspapers and on the radio! Gary shook his head

in amazement. "For the first time," he said to no one in particular, "it feels like we have a real band."

As the Galaxy One date approached, the band practiced hard. Mrs. Roesch made them understand how important this gig could be. Music critics from some of the papers would probably be there, along with important people from the record companies who normally hung out at the club. If they played well at Galaxy One, the word would spread and they'd be able to get other gigs at other good clubs.

When they weren't practicing, Gary and Susan were working on the new song Susan had written, or they were putting up the posters for the band on streetlight posts and on billboards already plastered with dozens of posters from other bands. Susan hardly went out at all. Mrs. Specter seemed very nervous. Gary asked her what the problem was and she said that there was so little to worry about that she was worried that she was missing something.

The day they were to play Galaxy One Gary tried to stay in bed until noon, but he was too excited and by nine he was up. Thomas was even more excited. Their parents had given him permission, to go to the club that night and this would be his first real gig as the band's official roadie and sound man. He was a transformed person— instead of wearing roller skates, tight jeans, and bright T-shirts, he now wore an old denim work-shirt and faded, baggy jeans with a pair of pliers in the back pocket and a roll of electrician's tape hanging from a belt loop.

Early that morning he'd put the band's equipment in the front hall, and about once an hour he went over it to make sure everything worked.

"It all works!" Gary finally yelled at him. "But if you keep fooling around with it you'll probably break something."

Thomas gave him a "What else am I supposed to do?" look, and Gary decided it was time they went out to the playground and shot some baskets.

When Gary, Susan, and Thomas arrived for the gig that night, they saw that Galaxy One had changed since the days only a few months before when it had been just a small, unknown club downtown. The club had expanded into the building next door and spotlights lit up the coming attractions announcements on the wall outside.

Even though it was still early, a large crowd of people was standing outside waiting to get in. While Gary and Thomas pulled the amps and guitars out of the cab, some of the crowd spilled over in their direction.

"You're not the Zoomies, are ya?" someone asked.

"No, we're the Coming Attractions."

"Never heard of ya!" someone yelled, and a couple of people laughed.

"You will after tonight!" Thomas yelled back. Roadie, record salesman, equipment repairman, and cheerleader.

Inside, the club had its own stage crew, who took the band's amps and other equipment and would set it up for them. In the meantime, Gary, Susan, and Thomas were directed to the dressing room upstairs.

Finally, a real dressing room. It was small, but it had couches and chairs and there were mirrors on the walls. Already there were guitar cases stacked against the couches and Gary assumed they belonged to members of the other bands. Pasted on the walls were publicity pictures and posters of the other bands who had played at the club and Thomas got out their poster and taped it up. A woman wearing a white blouse, black spandex slacks, and carrying a cocktail tray stuck her head in the door and asked if anyone wanted a drink, compliments of the management.

"I'll have a beer," Gary said.

"Me too," said Susan.

The woman looked at Thomas. He looked so young that Gary was amazed the waitress would serve him. "Can I get you something?" she asked.

"Got any martinis?" Thomas asked.

"I think he'd better stick to ginger ale," Gary told the waitress.

Thomas looked at Gary with disgust in his eyes. "I knew it," he snorted.

The waitress smiled. "I'll see what I can do," she said.

After she left, Gary turned to Susan. "What do you think?"

"I think we've made it," she replied.

"For tonight, at least," Gary said, chuckling.

The door of the dressing room opened again and Johnny Fantasy of the Zoomies walked in, carrying two guitar cases. Gary, Susan, and Thomas stared at him; Johnny stared back, but his eyes seemed to focus on Susan.

"Hi," he said.

"Hi," said Gary, Susan, and Thomas.

Johnny Fantasy put down his guitar cases and sat on the couch. He took a joint out of his pocket and lit it. Then he looked at Gary. "I'm Johnny Fantasy of the Zoomies," he said.

"Gary Specter of the Coming Attractions," Gary said.

"Susan Specter of the Coming Attractions," said Susan.

"Thomas Specter of the Coming Attractions," said Thomas.

Johnny Fantasy nodded. "A family happening, huh?"

"Well, Susan's my cousin and Thomas is the band's roadie," Gary explained.

"Dig it." Johnny Fantasy smiled at Susan.

"We're opening for you and the Ruptures," Gary said. "This is our first time in a big club."

"Oh, yeah?" Johnny said. He was now definitely

checking out Susan. "Well, this is a very happening club. It's a certified hot gig." He turned to Susan. "You sing?" he asked.

"And play bass," Susan said.

"No kidding?" Johnny Fantasy said, getting up and sitting next to her. "You want to meet our bass player?"

"Sure," Susan said.

Gary felt excluded from the conversation. He leaned toward Johnny. "Hey, you guys get signed yet?"

Johnny Fantasy slowly turned toward him. He was smiling, but it seemed to take an effort. "Yeah, we just signed with Roller Records. But we're gonna tour with the Usual Suspects before we cut an album." He turned back to Susan. "You know, we opened for them at the Palladium."

"Uh, is Roller Records a new company?" Gary asked.

Johnny Fantasy turned to Gary again. This time he wasn't smiling. "Yeah, pretty new." He turned back to Susan again. "You want to go downstairs for a drink?"

"Uh, you can get drinks up here, you know," Gary said.

Johnny Fantasy just ignored him. "Don't worry," he told Susan. "I'll make sure you're back in time for your set."

Susan got up and looked apologetically at Gary, but there was no rule that said she had to hang around in the dressing room before the show.

She and Johnny had hardly left when a couple of the Ruptures arrived and introduced themselves. Gary started talking to them. Soon Oscar, Karl, Randy, and Mrs. Roesch came, and then the waitress returned with some beers. She'd made up a glass of ginger ale with ice cubes, a slice of orange, and a swizzle stick for Thomas, and he sipped it as if it were a real drink. All of them sat around and made conversation with the Ruptures and their friends while the house photographer snapped pictures. It really did seem like the big time.

Half an hour before their set was to begin a stagehand came to the dressing room and told the band their equipment was ready on stage. In a way, Thomas was out of a job, but they said he could sit with the sound man during the set and be a "sound consultant."

The band was a neurotic bunch of nerves. Even Randy and Mrs. Roesch were jittery. Oscar, who'd been talking nervously since he'd arrived, put on his tuxedo and an old top hat he'd found somewhere. Karl seemed excited and held Randy's hand tightly. Together with Gary they reviewed the set list, switching and reswitching the order of the songs, mostly to kill time.

Finally Susan came back with Johnny Fantasy. Gary glanced at her anxiously. But what did he expect to see? He didn't know—he just had funny feelings.

Ten minutes to go. Gary's straitjacket drew

some funny looks from the other bands. Susan's low-cut red dress got some whistles and Johnny Fantasy wouldn't let her out of his sight. Getting into their show clothes, Gary felt the whole band calm down and get serious. Professionalism. That was the key. It didn't matter how much of a fool you were offstage—when the spotlights were shining you had to be pro-fes-sion-al.

Five minutes to go. Nervous conversations. Reassurances from the members of the other groups: "Don't worry, you'll knock 'em dead." "The guys on sound and lights are really good." "Tune up fast. Don't make the crowd wait."

Two minutes to go. A guy with a long brown ponytail and a thick mustache walked into the dressing room carrying a notebook. Everyone in the room except Gary and the Coming Attractions seemed to recognize him. "Hi, Mike!" "Hey, man." They all greeted him and Mike nodded back.

"Where's the Coming Attractions?" Mike asked.

"Here," Gary said. Susan was tying up his straitjacket. Mike scowled. "This part of your act or are you a new breed of dangerous musician?" he asked.

"Both," Gary answered.

That got a few laughs and then Mike introduced himself and Gary understood why everyone knew him. He was Mike Wexler of the *Voice*, the man whose rave reviews could make you an overnight sensation and get you a record contract.

One minute to go. "What are you, local New York kids?" Mike Wexler asked. He was jotting down some information in his notebook—names, ages, etc. Mrs. Roesch filled him in on all the details. As show time approached, Gary couldn't remember feeling so nervous or so excited. For the first time in his career as a performer, he'd started sweating even before the band went on stage.

Time. A stagehand carrying a small flashlight came for them. Gary and the rest of the group followed in single file out the door amid a flurry of "Good lucks" and "Knock 'em deads." They followed the stagehand down a hall and through a door, and suddenly they were in the dark, stepping gingerly around mounds of electronic equipment. Ahead of them they could hear loud taped rock music and the sounds of a crowd waiting.

With the stagehand's help they were able to find their places on the darkened stage. Karl had to adjust his drum set and Susan checked out her bass and Gary's guitar. Oscar's keyboard was on top of the ironing board, the microphones were live, and they could see the silhouettes of the audience and hear their conversations.

Then the stagehand stepped up to the mike: "Welcome to Galaxy One," he said to the audience. "Now, in their first appearance here, a local New York band, Gary Specter and the Coming Attractions Plus Oscar!"

The lights went on with a smattering of applause followed by the laughs and hoots that always came when a new audience discovered Gary in his straitjacket, Susan in her low-cut dress, and Oscar in his tuxedo at his ironing table. Gary started singing before the laughter died down.

> *"You know, they say I'm lazy,*
> *Don't want no responsibility . . ."*

They roared smoothly into "Rock Therapy," Karl's drums exploding, Susan thumping the bass, and Oscar's fingers racing over the keyboard. It was a good start, and as they went into the first chorus Susan started to untie the straitjacket.

Only, the straitjacket wouldn't come untied!

For a brief instant Susan and Gary looked at each other, terrified. But then it was time to start the second verse, and Gary jumped back to the mike, still bound in the jacket.

> *"My daddy wanted to send me to a shrink*
> *So that he could analyze the way that*
> *I think . . ."*

By now the rest of the band knew what had happened and they were trying to compensate. Oscar filled in the missing guitar solos with impromptu piano riffs, but with only a bass, piano and drums, the song sounded empty. Gary's heart sank to his toes. They'd botched up their first and best song.

By the end of "Rock Therapy," Thomas was waiting just offstage with a knife he'd borrowed from the bartender and he quickly cut the laces of the straitjacket. As they started their second song, Gary looked miserably at the rest of the band, but next to him Susan whispered, "It can only get better."

Three songs later it was better. Gary was in rock-and-roll heaven. There was no doubt about it, the audience was with them—hands slapping the tables, feet stomping the floor, laughing at the lyrics, applauding loudly at the end of each song. Even when one of Karl's cymbals fell over and Oscar's keyboard mysteriously went dead for a few moments, nothing could stop them. Had every piece of equipment they owned broken down that night, Gary was sure he could have had them screaming for a cappella.

The band roared through "Educated Fool" as they never had before. It was incredible. Susan was doing splits on the stage! Oscar left his keyboard and did something that resembled an Indian rain dance. Gary played on his knees. He felt like leaping off the stage and embracing the crowd in a giant hug. It was for them that he played, sang, screamed, twisted, twirled, grimaced, and cried. He wanted them, needed them, had to have them. They were his and he was theirs. He knew he could lie down on that stage and die for them!

Then the time came to play Susan's new song. Gary retreated from the front mike and Susan stepped up. She shook her hips provocatively at the crowd and began to sing:

> *"Once upon a time I used to stay out late*
> *With any man who would ask for a date.*
> *'Just pick me up,' I said. 'I'm always around,'*
> *But when they let me off, they always let*
> *   me down."*

Gary and Oscar joined her for the chorus:

> *"So keep your hands off me—*
> *I'm not what you think you see."*

Then Susan sang alone:

> *"Well, I've learned the rules.*
> *This girl's no fool."*

Then together the whole band sang:

> *"She's got a sex objection!"*

Susan sang the second verse:

> *"Now I'm not opposed to natural selection.*
> *Be true to me and I'll be sweet as confection.*
> *But try to make me part of some larger*
> *   collection.*

And you'll find I have a sex objection."

The crowd loved it. They laughed and cheered as Susan gyrated toward Oscar and then pretended to slap him when he ogled her. She sang:

"The sign says, 'Look but don't touch,'
'Cause this girl's been touched too much
And she's got a sex objection."

Fueled with audience support, the band bridged into solos and then came back for Susan's final verse:

"Now listen to me, girls.
If at night you're too easy,
In the morning you'll be queasy,
Till you have a sex objection."

Then, in one final chorus, the band joined together and sang:

"Till you have a sex objection!"

By the end of the song the crowd was applauding like mad. Susan was glowing and Gary invited her to share the front of the stage with him as they did their last number of the night, "I Fell in Love with the Baby-sitter." Susan's bass couldn't have been better.

And then suddenly—much too soon—it was

over. The stage went dark again, and even though Gary and the band had never received such loud stomping applause in their lives, they knew the set was finished and they felt sorry. The cheers felt good, but playing the music felt better. Gary was exhausted. Someone was tugging his arm and whispering, "Come on, we have to get off the stage." Gary reluctantly allowed himself to be pulled away.

But in the hallway offstage they were stopped. Gary didn't understand why. He was still in a daze. "Go back, go back," someone was whispering. "They want an encore." Gary allowed himself to be pushed back toward the stage.

Susan was shaking his arm. "What's wrong, Gary? What is it?"

Gary shook his head. "Nothing, nothing," he said. "What are we doing, an encore?" Gary was so giddy from all the excitement that he felt like laughing. Who could have guessed that anything like this could happen to them?

They were all back on the dark stage again, stumbling over things. The cheers from the crowd were almost deafening. Gary managed to plug his guitar into his amp. Oscar mentioned a song and Gary said, "But we've hardly practiced that."

Some people at the tables closest to the stage laughed. They'd heard him. *You're on stage now, birdbrain,* Gary told himself. By then Oscar had started playing and Gary just followed along. The spotlights came on again and Gary could see the rest of the band around him, soaked with sweat. Susan and Karl were grinning happily. Oscar was scowling at Gary as if to say, "Make it good!"

And they did. Gary gave it everything again. He didn't care if they had to carry him offstage on a stretcher. The only thing that mattered was the song. And the crowd. And the music.

Gary knew what was going on when the encore ended. He was so tired from playing and expending nervous energy that he could hardly stand up. And the crowd was on its feet, cheering!

Once again the band filed offstage in the dark, but again they were stopped. Behind them the rapid-fire chant of "More, more, more" rang in their ears. Ahead of them two people in the hall were arguing, but it was dark and Gary could only hear their voices.

"It's only an opening act, for God's sake!" said one.

"I don't care, send 'em back out," said the other.

"Listen, opening acts aren't even supposed to get first encores," the first one argued. "This stuff about second encores is nuts. I've got two other acts that have to play tonight."

"I said, send 'em out," the other insisted. "Worry about the other acts later."

The next thing Gary knew, they were heading back to the stage!

Oscar was yelling at them over the noise. "We do a two-minute version of 'Rock Therapy.' Short and loud." Then he turned to Gary. "You've got to say something to them before we start, Gary. Say thanks, tell them who we are. Talk to them."

This time the stage lights were left on when they went back and the crowd's cheers resurged. Gary stepped up to the microphone and the crowd grew quiet. He pushed some hair out of his eyes and grinned at them. "Well, uh," he said, scratching his head. "None of us here can figure out what's going on . . ."

The audience broke into laughter. The band laughed too, even though it was true. Gary waited for the laughter to die down. "But, we'd really like to thank you for being so, uh, nice." He didn't know what else to say. He glanced at Oscar, who was moving his lips frantically. "Oh, yeah," Gary said. "We're the Coming Attractions. I hope we can play again for you sometime."

And with that they broke into a short version of "Rock Therapy." Only this time Gary laced it with guitar riffs. The audience was on its feet again when the band left the stage for the last time.

In the hallway offstage the five members of the Ruptures were waiting to go on. As the two bands passed each other, Gary noticed that they didn't look very happy. Karl noticed it too, because he asked the stagehand who was leading them off about it.

"You guys upstaged 'em," the stagehand said. "They're gonna have to put on a damn good show to make the audience forget about you."

Gary beamed. He was thoroughly exhausted from the show, but too happy to care. People in the hallway stopped to congratulate them. Randy and Mrs. Roesch both tried to hug Karl. Finally they got back to the dressing room. All the Zoomies were there now and they eyed Gary and the band with a mixture of curiosity and resentment.

"Heard you put on a good show," Johnny Fantasy said.

Gary thanked him.

"Pity no one will remember it after our set," Johnny added. Some of the other Zoomies snickered.

Gary shrugged and went to sit with the rest of his band. A waitress came in with a tray filled with a selection of beverages and placed it on a table near the band. "Frank asked me to bring this up," the waitress told them. "He wants you to know he liked you a lot."

The band thanked the waitress and all of them reached for a beer or a soda. When the waitress was out of earshot, Susan said, "Who's Frank?"

Gary, Karl, and Oscar looked at each other. None of them knew.

Thomas joined them. "That other band stinks," he said.

Susan put her fingers to her lips and said, "Shush."

Gary was thinking about the show they'd just done. Around him, the other members of the band seemed to be in their own worlds. "We have to prepare our gigs better," Oscar said.

"Be quiet, Oscar," Susan told him. "Let us enjoy it for a while. We can talk about the problems tomorrow."

Johnny Fantasy came over and stood near them. He was looking at Susan and spoke to her as if the rest of the band didn't exist. "You gonna stay for our show?" he asked her.

"I might," Susan said.

"Then I might see you after it," Johnny said, grinning. He looked at the rest of the band. "Where are you guys playing next?"

"We don't know," Karl said.

"Well, you guys should get your act together and start playing the clubs regularly," Johnny said. "Who's your booking agent?"

"We don't have one," Gary said.

Johnny looked back at the other Zoomies, who were sitting across the room listening. "I'd tell you about ours," he said, "but I don't want to risk losing him." The Zoomies chuckled.

Now Mike Wexler stepped into the room. Johnny Fantasy saw him. "Hey, Mike, looking for the new phenoms?"

Mike Wexler came over and sat down with the band. He had a long thin pad of paper in one hand and a pen in the other. "I want to get some more on you kids," he told them.

Johnny tapped Wexler on the shoulder. "Hey, don't forget about us, huh?"

Mike Wexler looked up at the long-haired guitarist. "Who could forget you, Johnny?" he asked.

Johnny Fantasy smirked and walked away.

Mike turned back to the band. "I must tell you," he said seriously, "that was one of the most impressive debuts made by a band your age that I've seen in a long time. I think you kids are going to be a terrific act."

It was too good to be true. Mike Wexler talked to them for a while, and from his questions it was obvious that he was going to write a good review of their act. Finally he was finished. "Hey, good luck," he said, and left the band alone in the dressing room.

For a while no one spoke. It was like no one wanted to break the spell. Then Karl stood up, holding Randy's hand tightly. Mrs. Roesch stood up too.

"Well, guys," Karl said. "I guess we have to go. I still can't believe how great tonight was, but I have to tell you something. I'm, uh, going back to school next year. I still want to be in the band and everything, but I just want to warn you guys that I'll have to get some studying done too."

Everyone nodded.

Karl smiled. "Of course, if we get an offer to tour around the country, I might be willing to postpone the academics a little longer."

The band laughed and waved good-bye as the Roesch contingent left. Oscar got up next, holding the electronic keyboard under one arm and the ironing board under the other. "I just want you to know that I'm really glad to be a member of this band," he said, showing a rare smile. Then he kissed Susan on the cheek and left.

Susan shook her head in disbelief. "Was that really Oscar?" she asked.

"I guess," Gary said. Only he, Susan, and Thomas were left in the dressing room now, and Thomas was starting to yawn. "We better start packing up," Gary said, coiling up an amp cord. Susan went into another room and changed into her street clothes. Then she came back and helped them get ready to go.

"Aren't you gonna wait until Johnny Fantasy is through?" Gary asked.

Susan looked insulted. "Really, Gary—what kind of girl do you think I am?"

They picked up their guitar cases and Thomas went to get the amps. But as they left the dressing room Gary stopped and looked at the poster of Gary Specter and the Coming Attractions Plus Oscar that Thomas had stuck up on the wall.

"What is it, Gary?" Susan asked.

Gary turned to his cousin and his brother. "You know," he told them, "when we got off the stage for the last time tonight, I thought to myself, 'Wow, we finally made it!' Like all the time and work we've put into this band and all the dumb gigs we had to play and all the times we just wanted to cry—it was all worth it. We really did it tonight. *We were stars.*"

Susan and Thomas looked at each other. "I hate to remind him," Susan said to her little cousin, "but this was the gig he agreed to do for free."

"Yeah," Thomas told his brother. "I wouldn't get too excited. Mom's still gonna kill you if you don't get a summer job."

Susan and Thomas went downstairs, but Gary lingered in the dressing room a moment more, hating to leave.

ABOUT THE AUTHOR

TODD STRASSER is the author of two highly praised novels, *Angel Dust Blues* (available in a Dell Laurel-Leaf edition) and *Friends till the End*, published by Delacorte Press. His writing has appeared in many publications, including *The New Yorker* and *The Village Voice*. Mr. Strasser grew up on Long Island and now lives in New York City.